Radar Commandos

A Story of World War II

By BERNARD GLEMSER

Illustrated by George Avison

WINSTON
ADVENTURE
BOOKS

Cecile Matschat, *Editor*

Carl Carmer, *Consulting Editor*

THE JOHN C. WINSTON COMPANY

Philadelphia · Toronto

0121

For
Jonathan and Martin

The Radar Mission

IN World War II a struggle raged between the opposing forces that, in many ways, was more decisive than the battles fought between their massed armies—the struggle for technical supremacy. It was a struggle that brought to practical fulfilment such weapons as the jet plane, long-distance rockets and the atom bomb; yet these were all more complex forms of weapons that had been used in the earlier world war. The only new weapon to be used in World War II was radar.

Even the word itself is new, compounded from the descriptive term "radio detection and ranging." The principle of radar, strangely enough, was developed independently at roughly the same time by the United States,

England, France and Germany; but from the beginning the British saw in it the possibility of defense against aerial attack, to which their island was particularly vulnerable. They built their first experimental station in 1935. The United States was building successful equipment by the end of 1939; and in 1940 the two great nations began to work together to improve and extend the use of radar.

The earliest of the triumphs of radar was the defeat of the German night-bombing campaign against Britain. After this, its importance in warfare grew tremendously. Used on U.S. warships, for example, it was responsible for the sinking in one month of more than 100,000 tons of Japanese shipping in the Pacific Ocean—all at night, when the Japanese did not even suspect the presence of any striking force!

The British, naturally enough, were very sensitive to the use of radar by the Germans. In France, special Resistance agents reported constantly on the building of enemy radar installations. A keen eye was kept on these stations by Photographic Reconnaissance Unit planes, which photographed them regularly. This unceasing vigil resulted, eventually, in a major triumph for the Allies. Before the invasion fleet set sail for Europe on D-Day, a tremendous aerial onslaught was loosed against all the German radar stations on the invasion coast, resulting in the almost total destruction of the entire network. It was because of this that the invasion fleet was able to reach Normandy undetected and—of even greater importance—without terrible loss of life.

The raid on Bruneval occurred in 1942, when the vital secret of radar was being carefully guarded by both sides. It was the first time in history, perhaps, that a task force was sent into enemy territory on a scientific mission; and it was repeated later in the war when, fearing German experiments that seemed to be leading toward the atom bomb, another task force destroyed an installation in Norway suspected of manufacturing heavy water.

The young hero of this story, Paul Martin, is of course fictitious; but he can stand as a symbol of the many courageous young Frenchmen who worked so selflessly for their country throughout the years of occupation. Sergeant Gaston Villard and Captain Dubois are fictitious too, and yet not altogether fictitious; for there were thousands of men like them, serving France under the most tragic and dangerous circumstances. And the commandos were very real, as the Nazis discovered.

For obvious reasons the names of living persons concerned with the raid on Bruneval have been changed in this narrative. The officer in command of the airborne troops was Major J. D. Frost, of the Cameronians. Mention should also be made of Flight-Sergeant Cox, R.A.F., who was responsible for dealing with the radar installation.

An account of the raid is contained in *Combined Operations: The Official Story of the Commandos,* published in 1943 by the Stationery Office in London. (New York, The Macmillan Co.)

B. G.

CONTENTS

xi

CHAPTER 1

The Fire Bowl

Paul Martin was on forbidden territory when the mystery plane came screaming across the sky, and in those few seconds he nearly lost his life.

Paul knew perfectly well that he was not allowed to approach within half a mile of the farm. Anybody who did so was liable to be shot on sight. It was guarded by fifteen machine-gun posts and more than a hundred soldiers. An entire regiment was encamped nearby, and a few miles farther on, there was an armored car battalion which could swoop down on the farm at tremendous speed in case of trouble. Night and day, fighter planes circled around watchfully like hawks. To cross the barbed-wire boundaries and ignore the signs that said KEEP OUT must have seemed like madness.

But Paul was not mad. He had his own good reasons for defying the orders to keep away.

The farm had not always been like this: mysterious, menacing, guarded by armed soldiers. Until a little more than a year and a half ago he had been free to play there whenever he pleased. *Le Presbytère,* as the farm was called, had been a wonderful place. It was surrounded by woods, and Paul knew every path, every tree, every rabbit hole. Better still, it was only a few hundred yards from the sea, and he passed by it whenever he went down to the beach to swim or fish. The farmer's wife would call out to him and give him some of her delicious homemade candy or let him sample the cookies she had just baked. He was as welcome at the farm as he was in his own home.

Until a little more than eighteen months ago . . .

Until May, 1940, early in World War II, when the Germans smashed through the defenses of France and overran the country.

Paul was a typical French boy of fifteen, strong and wiry, with brown eyes and a fine face. Like all French boys, he burned with love of his land. When the Germans defeated the proud French armies he felt as if his heart was broken. But that was not the only tragedy the war had brought to him. His father, a major in the French air force, was reported missing in action. His mother became sick and was taken to a hospital in some distant place where he could not go to visit her.

For a time he was alone, until a relative named Theo Leblanc came to live in the house. He was a tall, quiet man who had been badly wounded in the war and walked with a cane, and Paul soon adored him.

Then the Nazis arrived in the village—the peaceful little village of Bruneval. They occupied the farm, ordering the farmer and his family to leave, and threw a barbed-wire fence around it. The farmer had just built a house on the cliffs which he hoped to rent to summer visitors, and the Nazis took this too. The big

ugly signs were put up everywhere: KEEP OUT. The machine-gun nests and concrete pillboxes were hurriedly built. And then all the strange, secret things began to happen.

It was Theo who asked Paul to keep an eye on all the things that were going on at the farm. "It is vital that we should know what they are doing," Theo said, and Paul did not question whom Theo meant by *we*. There was no need for explanation. Whether the Germans liked it or not, the French people were still in the battle for freedom. They had been vanquished, but the war was not yet over.

So Paul watched all the strange secret activities at the farm. He knew how to reach it by a hundred different paths; he knew every hollow in which he could hide, every bush that would conceal his slender body.

This is what he saw:

First, the Germans turned the farmhouse into a barrack, in which the soldiers slept and ate their meals.

At the same time, they began to work on the house on the cliffs.

Near this house—between the house and the cliffs—they dug a big circular pit. This was connected by deep, narrow trenches to the house and to various machine-gun posts.

Around the edge of the pit they built a thick concrete wall, and in the center a massive concrete platform.

A convoy of big trucks arrived with complicated machinery and a great many gray steel boxes. They brought, too, the monstrous thing that Paul called the Fire Bowl. It was like a huge electric bowl heater, ten or twelve feet in diameter, and he could think of no other name by which to call it. So it was always called the Fire Bowl.

Then he saw the Fire Bowl mounted on the heavy concrete platform in the circular pit. As week after week went by, it became clear that all the precautions the Germans were taking, all the machine guns, all the soldiers and all the armored cars and all the Luftwaffe fighter planes circling overhead—all were there to protect the Fire Bowl. Nothing else. This

project was so secret, so vital, that the Germans were going to fantastic lengths to protect it.

But what was it? What was the Fire Bowl meant to do?

Paul could not even guess. He watched it from behind tree trunks in the woods and saw it being tested, but his bewilderment only increased. He saw it revolve slowly. He saw it tilt gently in the air and turn as it tilted. He saw it turn swiftly and then stop without a tremor.

He heard the hum of generators, and occasionally the harsh crackle of electricity, like static. He saw German officers and technicians huddling over blueprints and books. He saw, also, that the machine guns were always on the alert, always searching the skies.

All this he reported faithfully to Theo. Every morning at dawn he would go stealthily to the woods and watch; and when he returned Theo would be waiting.

"But what is this machine?" Paul asked Theo one day. "What is it supposed to do?"

Theo's eyes narrowed. "I can't answer your question," he said gravely, "because I don't know. I have never seen anything like it. But I know this—it's meant to harm our Allies."

"Then we should tell them about it," Paul exclaimed.

"Should we?" Theo laughed.

"Yes!"

"Perhaps you're right," Theo said. "But

that's something I don't want you to worry
about."

"Why?"

"Because the job you are doing is dangerous enough," Theo said quietly. "It would be
very serious if the Germans caught you now,
but if they found out that you were passing on
any information about the Fire Bowl to the
Allies it would be disastrous. So it is better for
you to be ignorant about this and not to ask
too many questions."

There was no need for Paul to ask any more
questions. Theo's words made him realize that
his work was important and in a great cause.
Everything he reported to Theo about this
amazing Fire Bowl would, somehow, help the
Allies and would in God's own time help to
bring freedom and peace to his beloved
country.

On the morning the mystery plane came
over, Paul left his home, as usual, at dawn. It
was late in January, and there had been a thin
sprinkling of snow during the night; but the

clouds were already lifting and Paul could tell that the day was going to be cold and clear.

He went cautiously through the village, carrying a sack under his arm so that if anybody saw him they would assume that he was going out to snare rabbits. All the villagers did the same, for ever since the Germans came to Bruneval there had been a shortage of food.

He took one of his secret trails through the woods, moving as quietly as possible and avoiding patches of snow to prevent his footsteps being discovered. For some reason he felt a little uneasy this morning, and he was extra careful. He crept from tree to tree, his body low, pausing constantly to listen for any sound of danger—the crackle of twigs, the sudden cry of an alarmed bird. Even though the woods were still and quiet Paul had this foreboding of danger, and his skin tingled as if he were being watched. Once or twice he had an urge to run back to the safety of his home.

He tried to laugh at his fears and urged himself on until he reached his favorite vantage point, only a few hundred yards from the farmhouse. The trees at this point narrowed into a thin spur, and he could watch all the Nazis' activities from here. He had one special spot which gave him a perfect view of the Fire Bowl—a little embankment with a deep hollow in the top which might have been made to measure for him.

He had just reached it, wriggling flat along the ground, when a harsh voice snapped, "On your feet, Frenchman."

His blood ran cold. For a moment the shock was so great that he could not move. Then, very slowly, he stood up, and a soldier in a field-gray uniform came out from behind a tree, rifle leveled menacingly at Paul's head. There was a loud crackling in the undergrowth, and other Nazis sprang out, their guns ready for action in case he attempted to run. They had been hiding here, Paul realized; they had been waiting silently to ambush him.

"But he's only a boy!" one of the soldiers cried.

The first soldier growled. "He's still a spy. Search him."

Paul tried to control his fear. He knew how the Nazis punished anybody suspected of spying, and it made no difference whether the spy was fifteen years old or fifty.

He held out the canvas sack he had been carrying under his arm and said in a bold, blustering voice, "I haven't done anything wrong. I was only looking for rabbits."

"Tell that to the Camp Commandant. We saw you here yesterday morning, but you got away before we could lay our hands on you. You won't get away this time, though."

He was searched roughly and then ordered to march ahead. There was no possibility of escape; the three soldiers followed too closely. They would have mowed him down before he had covered ten yards.

The little group came out of the woods into the open fields, heading for the farmhouse, when suddenly Paul heard the whine of a plane. The three soldiers heard it at the same moment and stopped nervously to look up at the sky. The whine grew louder and louder until it was a mighty scream that made the air

tremble, and then Paul saw it head-on, flying low and at tremendous speed directly toward him.

"Spitfire!" one of the soldiers shouted, and all three flung themselves on the ground. The British Spitfires were the most deadly of all planes then operating, and they usually carried eight machine guns, four in each gracefully curved wing. The Nazis had learned through bitter experience what terrible havoc these planes could inflict.

Paul stood half-paralyzed, watching it zoom like an arrow over the field, over Le Presbytère, over the Fire Bowl. He saw the R.A.F. roundels on each wingtip and waited for the machine guns to begin their frightful clatter. For some reason it did not fire, although the machine-gun posts on the cliff opened up wildly, and it went whistling out to sea. It had come and gone with only a great crescendo of noise to mark its passing.

Yet in those few seconds Paul noticed something he had not seen before. The Fire Bowl had turned silently on its concrete base, following the plane's course. It had turned as the Spitfire flew over it! The fact registered almost subconsciously on his dazed mind.

At the same instant he realized that he was no longer covered by the rifles of his captors. They were still flat on the ground, evidently expecting other Spitfires to fly over. At once he turned and sprinted for the woods. It was his only chance. He ran in a wild zigzag, bent double, but before he reached cover the bullets were whining around him and he felt something rip across his right arm like the point of a red-hot needle. Gasping, he plunged into the woods and ran until he could go no further. Then he sank down in a brier patch, exhausted.

After some time he heard noises in the distance. The Nazis were searching for him. Miraculously, they did not search long. There was a long piercing whistle from the direction of the farmhouse; it was repeated several times and then the woods became quiet. He wondered what had happened, and a possible explanation occurred to him. Presumably the Nazis had been alarmed by the appearance of the Spitfire, and every available man had been recalled to guard the Fire Bowl.

For more than an hour Paul stayed where he was, not daring to move. The wound in his arm, he discovered, was not serious; the bullet had only grazed the flesh without drawing blood, and there were two small holes in the sleeve of his jacket where the bullet had passed through.

Eventually he began to make his way home. He crept through the woods as warily as a fox. When he reached the village he went around the back yards of the houses in order to avoid being seen.

Theo was waiting for him anxiously. The tall man listened without any comment as Paul told the story of being captured and of the Spitfire flying over at the critical moment.

"Yes," Theo said, when Paul finished. "I heard the plane. It's unusual for only one to fly over like that; they nearly always fly in some kind of formation. The Nazis must be wondering whether this one came here on purpose or by accident. They will be on the alert from now on. But there's something of even greater importance that concerns you."

"What?" Paul asked.

"A Nazi motorcycle patrol is searching for a young Frenchman who escaped from military custody this morning. He was caught spying on Le Presbytère and they're determined to find him. I heard this news from our good village gendarme, who is supposed to be assisting in the search."

"I certainly made a mess of everything today," Paul said weakly.

"You've done a magnificent job," Theo said, and suddenly gripped Paul's shoulder. There was the explosive rattle of a military motorcycle in the street outside, and the man and the boy stood listening grimly as it approached. But it went on, without stopping.

"There isn't a minute to be lost," Theo said. "Paul, you must go into hiding immediately."

Paul stared at him, white-faced. "But where can I hide?"

"In the caves beyond the village," Theo said. "The Nazis haven't discovered them yet. You will stay there until I make arrangements for your safety."

"What arrangements?" Paul asked.

"You will see. But don't be scared. You'll hear from me very quickly." He took Paul's arm. "Let's go."

The intelligence officer greeted him cheerfully. "Hello, there! Did you have a good flight?"

The pilot grinned. "Pretty good. Hitler's Europe was blessed with perfect visibility this morning."

"Fine. Did you get all your targets?"

"I hope so." The pilot pulled a map from the knee pocket of his flying suit, spread it on the table and pointed to several points which he had encircled with red pencil. "I covered each of these," he said. Then he dotted in a pencil line showing his route across France, into Germany and back to the airfield.

"Did you meet any opposition anywhere?"

"A couple of Messerschmitts tried to tag me, but I ran like a bunny and they didn't give me any more trouble."

"Good. Did you happen to spot anything interesting apart from your targets?"

"Well," the pilot said, and hesitated. He pointed to a spot on the map. "This is where I came out of France on my way back."

"Bruneval," the intelligence officer said. "Just a small village, isn't it?"

"Yes. But it seemed to me that there was some queer gadget up on the cliffs there. Something like a big searchlight. I was flying at zero feet and full throttle to avoid the local machine-gun crews, so I didn't have much time to see it clearly; but my camera was running and there's just a chance that it may register on my last exposures."

"I'll look at the prints as soon as they're ready," the intelligence officer said. "It's worth reporting to headquarters, though. I'll make a note of it."

Every detail was worth reporting. A searchlight—if it was a searchlight—meant that the Nazis had some fear of Allied action in that area. They might be building a new anti-aircraft site there, or developing it as a training ground for special troops. Whatever it was, it indicated activity that should be reported and investigated if necessary.

In a short while the photographs arrived on the intelligence officer's desk—a pile of about seventy black and white prints, each roughly about four inches square. He went through them rapidly, checking off the targets. They had all been photographed with perfect precision, as if the pilot had stopped in mid-air to set up his camera on some aerial tripod instead of speeding across them at more than three hundred and fifty miles an hour. After the last target there was merely a series of pictures showing long stretches of countryside, which was normal in these circumstances. When a pilot finished photographing his targets he was instructed to keep his camera running until he left enemy territory; sometimes these random shots provided useful information.

The last two shots in this series showed a house on a cliff, taken—as the pilot had said—from a low altitude. The officer looked at them curiously and saw what the pilot had described—a circular object that looked like a large searchlight. This object stood in a pit near the house, with woods in the background. As a matter of interest, the officer put the two photographs under his stereoscope, a simple metal frame holding two spectacle lenses, standing on four thick wire legs. The effect was peculiar. The house and the woods stood up in vivid relief, as if the officer were looking down at the living scene. Near the woods, in fact, he could see some tiny figures lying on the ground—Nazi soldiers. For some reason, though, the circular object was blurred, and it was impossible to tell its exact shape. All that he could see for certain was that it was round, black, and connected to the house by lines which indicated newly dug cable trenches.

For a minute or so he was puzzled by the photographs. The blurring of the circular object was very strange. This was an effect that happened only because of movement. A car in motion, for example, would photograph and register under the stereoscope as a blur; so would a running man. The blur meant that the object had moved appreciably between the taking of the two pictures. Yet it looked solid enough, anchored to a concrete platform.

He made a notation on his report: *Unidentified object on prints 68 and 69. Photographed over Bruneval, 12 miles NNE of Le Havre, N. France.* A few minutes later a motorcycle dispatch rider came to his office, collected the prints and the report, and went thundering off with them to the heart and brain of all these activities—Allied Intelligence Headquarters.

Late that afternoon an R.A.F. officer sat studying the two photographs—prints 68 and 69. He was a middle-aged man with a strong, handsome face. On the sleeves of his uniform were the rings denoting the rank of squadron leader. His name was Marshall. He wore rimless spectacles, and attached to one lens was an additional small magnifying glass. He bent low over his desk, examining through this small powerful lens the circular object near the house on the cliff, first in one photograph and then in the other. He examined both together under his stereoscope, and stared at the vividly realistic scene for a long time. After a

while he took a pair of dividers and a slide rule and began to measure the object, and then to make a number of calculations. Finally, frowning, he took the two photographs and walked out of his room and along a narrow corridor, entering another office where a uniformed girl sat peering through a stereoscope.

He said briefly, "Mary, I'd like you to look at these," and put the photographs on her desk.

Her name was Mary Collier, and she was one of the most brilliant officers in this branch of the R.A.F. She smiled at Marshall, placed the photographs under her stereoscope, looked at them for a few moments, examined them separately, and said in a quiet voice, "Yes. The thing in the pit is blurred. Everything else is sharp, though."

"Right," Marshall said. "You know what that means?"

"It must have moved between the two exposures."

"Exactly. It turned on its base while the

camera plane flew over it. *It followed the course of the plane in flight.*"

She leaned back thoughtfully. "Very interesting," she said. "Very interesting indeed. It couldn't be a searchlight, because nobody in his senses would use a searchlight in broad daylight. And yet . . . Have you measured it, squadron leader?"

"It's about twelve feet in diameter, as near as I can tell. Possibly a little smaller."

"A twelve-foot, bowl-shaped reflector that can follow a plane flying at three hundred and fifty miles an hour," Mary Collier said gravely. "Could a gadget of this kind be hooked up to control anti-aircraft guns?"

"That's what I'm afraid of," Marshall said. "Have you seen anything like this before?"

"No," she answered. She clasped her hands together tightly. Her eyes had become very serious. "Squadron leader," she said, "I think you should show these photographs to the commanding officer immediately."

"I think you're right," Marshall said.

* * * * *

The commanding officer of Intelligence Headquarters was Group Captain Smith, a man of the same age as Marshall, very tall and thin. He listened to Marshall's remarks about the two photographs, studied them through his stereoscope, and then blinked once or twice.

"Unidentified object," he said, and laughed. He picked up the photographs and stared at them earnestly.

"Marshall," he said in a strained voice, "this thing looks like the most serious menace we've discovered so far. According to what you've already learned from the pictures, it picked up the track of one of our fastest planes, a reconnaissance Spitfire. It followed this plane in flight. Therefore, anybody operating this machine could have telephoned or radioed that information to a nearby anti-aircraft battery, couldn't they?"

"Yes, sir."

The commanding officer continued grimly,

"In fact, it wouldn't be too difficult to hook up this machine so that it automatically controlled the fire of a battery of anti-aircraft guns. Do you agree?"

"I do, sir. That's what is worrying me."

"There's plenty to worry about, Marshall. If it can track a fast Spitfire like this, it can certainly track a formation of relatively slow-moving bombers."

"Yes, sir. And it could then not only control anti-aircraft fire but alert enemy fighter squadrons in the area."

The group captain looked at Marshall for some time without speaking. Then he said, "This is going to have the most serious effects on our entire air strategy, squadron leader. It could play havoc with all our plans for the next two years."

"Do the Allies have such a device, sir?"

For a few seconds the commanding officer did not answer. "Yes," he said finally in a quiet voice. "We do have such a device. It's considered such a vital secret that even officers like yourself haven't been told about it yet. It helped to stop the German air fleets from bombing us into defeat." He paused. "These photographs are the first indication that the Germans have this same device. And it could very well prevent us from liberating Europe."

He picked up a telephone on his desk and pressed a button. When his orderly answered he said, "Get me Air Commodore Simpson at the Air Ministry on the scrambler. Most urgent. I'll hold on until he comes through."

He was connected almost at once.

"For immediate consideration, sir," he said. "I have in front of me two photographs taken this morning over Bruneval, twelve miles NNE of Le Havre. These photographs make it appear likely that the Nazis have *carrots*."

Marshall was startled by the statement, but the man at the other end of the telephone was even more startled. There was an exclamation of surprise, and then a babble of questions.

"Yes, sir," the group captain said. "The circular bowl type . . . near the sea . . . protected by machine guns . . ."

More anxious questions.

Finally the commanding officer said quietly, "Yes, sir. I'll send the photographs over to you at once by dispatch rider." He replaced the telephone and looked at Marshall.

"The Nazis are growing carrots," he said cryptically. "You'd better stand by for further developments."

CHAPTER 3

In the Caves

PAUL slept that night in the caves of Bruneval, for the first and last time in his life. Unlike some of the caves in the mountainous regions of France which go hundreds of feet down through the earth and were used as shelters by prehistoric man, these were small and almost on the surface. Few people outside of Bruneval knew about them; only by sheer bad fortune could they ever have

34

been discovered by the Nazis. The entrance was under a large boulder and screened by bushes, a slit scarcely large enough to allow a man's body through. But for centuries the boys of Bruneval had been climbing in and out of this hole, and so—in the past eighteen months—had a number of men of different nationalities, French, British, Canadian, American, Polish. Inside, on one of the walls, these men had inscribed their names, as if in a visitors' book. They were Allied soldiers and fliers who had been brought here by the gallant French Resistance, hiding for a night or two in the course of escaping from the Germans.

In a rather crude fashion the caves were furnished and fit for human habitation. There were boards covered with sacks of straw, to serve as beds; wooden boxes for chairs and tables; tin cups and saucers, a stock of candles, and even a small library of books and magazines. "The best hotel in town," somebody had scribbled on the wall.

Paul slept restlessly, however. His mind was

filled with thoughts of the Fire Bowl, and he dreamed about it all night long. He dreamed of it as he had seen it early that morning when the German soldiers had captured him—a huge copper bowl facing up to the sky, turning like something evil as the Spitfire swept overhead. In his dream it shot out great streamers of flame, scorching the Spitfire so that it fell helplessly into the sea. Then he dreamed that there were Fire Bowls all over France, and everywhere they were doing the same—turning, tilting, reaching out with fingers of flame at every Allied aircraft in the sky and bringing them crashing down. It was very frightening to Paul as he slept; for how would his beloved country be liberated now? How could the Allies drive the Nazis out of France if the Fire Bowls destroyed the British and American air fleets?

He woke early, climbed cautiously out of the entrance to the caves, and stood for a little while breathing in the cold, fresh morning air. The sky was glowing with the colors of dawn, and he felt is if he were alone in the world. A few crows were cawing far off in the fields, and the robins were already busily searching for their breakfast; and Paul was glad of their company. A small stream trickled through the rocks nearby and he made his way to it and washed. The water was icy, but after the first shock he felt it warming his blood. Then he went back to the caves, but just before he reached the entrance he stopped in alarm. Ahead of him there was the patter of footsteps.

His first impulse was to run. He was sure the Germans had discovered his hide-out. It was hard to fight down the feeling of panic that came over him, but he did. Listening carefully, he realized that the footsteps were those of one person walking quickly and lightly, as if on tiptoe. The Nazis never walked like this. They walked heavily, arrogantly, and usually in pairs. One Nazi would never dare to come alone to a deserted place like the caves.

Even so, it was necessary to be careful. The Nazis had corrupted some Frenchmen to act as spies, as informers, as decoys; whoever was walking ahead might be one of these despised betrayers, a collaborator.

Scarcely daring to breathe, Paul crept forward. Then, at the boulder that covered the entrance to the caves, he caught sight of the intruder. To his astonishment he saw that it was a girl wearing a gray raincoat and a black

beret. He heard her voice, low and musical, calling, "Paul! Paul Martin!" He hesitated for a moment and then stepped out from the bushes in which he had been concealed.

She whirled around, startled. For two or three seconds they stared at each other, and suddenly she smiled and held her hand out to him in a gesture of friendship. "Paul," she said. "You must be Paul. Theo sent me here."

"Who?" Paul asked, watching her eyes.

"Theo Leblanc."

"Why did he send you here?" Paul asked. He was still guarded, suspicious.

She came close to him and put her hand reassuringly on his arm. "You can trust me," she said. "We are friends and allies in the same cause. My name is Denise Chausson. I am from the Resistance."

"The Resistance!" It was a magical name, which brought warmth and hope to any loyal Frenchman's heart. The Resistance was the secret army of France, a force of blazingly patriotic men and women who had sworn to continue the fight against the invaders until

France was free again. They were armed only with the guns that the Allies dropped for them by parachute at night, or which they stole in daring raids on Nazi arsenals. It was partly because of the Resistance that the Nazis were forced to keep large garrisons in the country.

"Yes," the girl said quietly. "The Resistance sent me because you're in danger here. I have instructions to take you to a safer place."

"The Nazis will never find me in these caves," Paul said.

She turned her head abruptly, as if she had caught some distant sound. She held her hand up and said, "Listen!"

Paul heard, far away, the yelping of dogs. The noise was very faint, but it made him shiver.

"Bloodhounds," Denise said.

She began to speak quickly. "Paul, the Nazis are anxious to catch you. They're afraid that you may know too much about their Fire Bowl on the cliffs. Last night I arrived at your house and spoke to Theo about taking you to safety. It's vitally important that you shouldn't be captured by the Germans, for your own sake as well as for ours. I'll explain more later, but in the meantime you must trust me." She looked at her wrist watch. "Do you know the farmer who owns the farm a mile away from here? Monsieur Durand?"

"Yes."

"In ten minutes' time he will be driving his wagon along the little road that leads to Angerville. He'll be alone. If everything is safe for us he'll be smoking his pipe. At the turn of the road, by the old disused barn, he'll stop for a few seconds to tighten his horse's harness. That will be the signal for us to climb into the wagon. Now, are you ready?"

"Yes," Paul said. "I just have to get my coat and the food I've left down in the cave."

"Never mind the food. Hurry and get your coat. We have to get to the barn exactly on time; otherwise we might be caught by the Nazi patrol car."

Paul left her without another word, slipped down into the cave and returned with his coat.

He was gone less than a minute, and she smiled gratefully.

"Which way are you going?" he asked.

"Down this path and across the fields there."

"No," he said. "I know a short cut. Along here." They set off, and he asked, "You're a stranger in Bruneval, aren't you?"

"Yes, I am," she answered.

"How do you know so much about M. Durand, and his wagon, and the barn?"

"It was all arranged by Theo," Denise said. "As you know, he's one of our leaders in this area."

Paul laughed. "I didn't know. But I guessed that he was."

"He's a fine man," Denise said. "He's done some magnificent work for us."

They hurried over the hard, wintry ground. The noise of bloodhounds was coming nearer, a terrifying sound, but Paul had faith in this girl who had come up to the caves and sought him out. He led her through a dense copse; then, when they reached the Angerville road he went along a shallow ditch under the cover of rows of poplar trees. They just had time to duck behind the old barn when the Nazi patrol car roared past.

"Whew!" Paul said.

"Don't worry," Denise said. "It won't come along this road again for another two hours."

Then Paul heard the heavy rumble of the farmer's wagon, the slow clip-clop, clip-clop of a horse's hoofs. Peering round the side of the barn, he saw the wagon stop and M. Durand climbing down in a leisurely way to fix the harness. He was a big man with a red, cheerful face and an enormous waxed mustache, and he was smoking a small pipe with a clay bowl that seemed designed to keep his nose warm. It was hard to believe that his casual, unhurried movements on the road were part of a carefully laid plan.

"Let's go," Denise whispered.

They seemed to cover the distance from the barn in a flash. Then, in a swift scramble, they were both over the side of the wagon, smiling at each other amid piles of vegetables. At the same time the farmer had climbed back into his seat and was clucking at his horse. As the wagon creaked forward he called in a low, chuckling voice, "Very good, my young friends. Very good. Now hide yourselves under the tarpaulin and take care you do not squash too many of my cabbages."

"The bloodhounds won't find you here," Denise laughed.

She had pulled the tarpaulin up so that they were both covered by it, yet had plenty of air circulating; and Paul felt very cosy and almost contented. It was all a strange, confusing adventure and he had no idea how it was going to end or even what was going to happen next, but he was not frightened in any way. He had infinite trust in all these people who had taken him so decisively into their charge.

The warmth and the slow jogging of the wheels rumbling over the rough road made him sleepy, and he drowsed off, vaguely wondering how Theo would get along without him, whether Theo would write to his mother and tell her that he had left Bruneval, and who would now get the information about the

Fire Bowl. He began to dream all over again about the Spitfire; and, quite suddenly, he woke, frightened. Denise had clutched his arm and was saying, "Don't worry. Don't worry. It's all right—"

There was a lurch as the wagon stopped, and voices were shouting violently in the road. The tarpaulin was pulled away, and Paul found himself staring at two men in Nazi uniform who were pointing their rifles at him.

"Out," one of the men commanded. "And hurry. We don't have all day to waste."

Mechanically, Paul climbed out of the wagon and saw that a gray Nazi patrol car was drawn across the road, with a third Nazi sitting at the wheel. He glanced at Denise and saw that she was calm and unworried; and his suspicions returned. Had she betrayed him to the Nazis, after all?

"Into the car," the soldier ordered. "Double-quick!"

They all crowded into the car, and it spun forward with a scream of tires. The soldier turned to Denise and asked gruffly, "Is this

youngster Paul Martin?" To Paul's consternation she replied, "Yes." He felt a pang of bitterness at being captured so easily, without a fight, without a chance to show his hatred for the enemies of his country; and he began to say furiously, "You Nazis will never conquer us. Never . . ."

"Be quiet, young man," the soldier said calmly. "You will have plenty of opportunity to speak your mind in a little while."

The driver kept the throttle wide open, tearing along at top speed as all the Nazi patrols did. He roared through a Nazi checkpoint, where all cars were supposed to stop for inspection, with a wave of his hand at the guards; passed a second check-point in the same way; then without diminishing speed turned recklessly off the main road down a narrow lane. The car bounced so violently that Paul could hardly keep his seat, even though he was wedged between Denise and the soldier. It was a nightmarish drive, as if the driver had no interest in the safety of his passengers and was interested only in covering the greatest distance in the least possible time. There was something particularly frightening about it, too, for both soldiers—the one in the front seat beside the driver, and the one beside Paul—kept their rifles at the alert, as if they expected at any moment to run into danger.

The danger never came.

Suddenly the car swung off the road, onto a gravel path leading to a large house. As it slowed down, the soldier sitting beside Paul took off his battle helmet, clapped Paul on the shoulder, and said triumphantly, "We made it! We made it!"

Denise was smiling happily. She said, "Here we are, Paul."

He looked at her and then at the soldiers. "What is this?" he stuttered. "What's happening?"

The soldier laughed. "To get you away

from the Nazis we had to *become* Nazis for a little while. How do you think we could have taken you through all those check-points in broad daylight otherwise? They stop every car, every bicycle, every little dog. So we had to wear these vile uniforms."

The driver turned and grinned at Paul. "Glad to have you with us, young fellow. I hope you enjoyed the drive." Then he said to Denise, "You'd better hurry. The captain is waiting."

"Come," Denise said, and touched Paul's arm.

He stumbled out of the car and followed her. He just had time to see the car swing round, drive toward a clump of trees, and disappear among them as if the earth had swallowed it up.

CHAPTER 4

"London Is Waiting"

THERE WAS a broad balcony running all
the way round the house, and as Denise
led Paul up the steps to the front door
his eyes nearly popped out with astonishment.
Half a dozen old ladies were sitting in rocking
chairs, bundled up in woolen jackets and
shawls, busily knitting and chatting to each
other. They looked frail, but rosy-cheeked and
happy, as if they thoroughly enjoyed sitting
50

out in the cold morning air. Inside the house
there was a throng of them, some in wheel
chairs, some attended by nurses in starched
uniforms, some reading or sewing or playing
cards. They did not seem to find it at all
strange that into their midst should come a
breathless young man and a girl in a raincoat
and beret.

"What is this place?" Paul whispered to
Denise.

"Exactly what it appears to be," she replied,
smiling. "A home for old ladies."

"The Resistance . . . in an old ladies'
home!"

"Why not? You're surprised. The Nazis
would be even more surprised. And it's the
last place in which they'd dream of looking
for us. What is more, the old ladies are great
patriots and help us in a thousand different
ways."

He had expected some kind of under-
ground fortress, heavily armed and guarded
by tough men with Tommy guns. This peaceful scene was totally unexpected. But as soon

as he thought about it he chuckled inwardly.
It would be difficult to think of a more perfect
hide-out. Even an entire regiment of Nazis
would be intimidated at the sight of fifty or
sixty spry old ladies shouting defiance at them.

Denise led him up two flights of stairs and
tapped at a door marked MATRON. A
woman's voice said, "Come in," and Denise

opened the door quietly and entered. The matron was sitting at her desk making entries in a large book. She glanced up, nodded, and continued with her work. Denise walked across the room, out into a narrow passage, and then up a flight of steep stairs which led to the attic. There was another door here with a heavy padlock on it. She knocked three times, and the door openedly silently, complete with the padlock, which was attached to a false upright.

The room was like most attics, filled with large trunks, packing cases and discarded furniture. One corner had been cleared, though. Here there were two tables. At one, covered with radio apparatus, sat a man wearing headphones and scribbling on a writing pad. At the other sat a man of about thirty, with a dark handsome face and very broad shoulders. He smiled warmly as Paul and Denise entered, but the first thing Paul noticed about him was the tiredness in his eyes. He looked as if he had not slept for a month.

Denise said, "Captain, this is Paul Martin. Paul, I want you to meet Captain Dubois, who is in command of our sector."

The captain stood up and held his hand out. "Welcome, Paul. I've heard a great deal about you, and it's a pleasure to meet you at last." He turned to Denise. "I hope you didn't run into any trouble coming here?"

"The arrangements worked perfectly," she answered. "We drove through the Nazi checkpoints at ninety miles an hour—or at least that's how it felt." She laughed and then became serious. "There's only one complication. The Nazis are looking for Paul in earnest. They are using their bloodhounds."

The captain frowned, and his fingers drummed on the table. "They must be a bundle of nerves," he said. "It's clear that this whole business is much more important than we suspected." He made a gesture toward the radio apparatus. "The radio is practically red-hot. We've had messages coming over from London all night. Neither Philippe nor I got a wink of sleep."

He smiled at Paul. "Sit down, lad. I want to talk to you. Denise, you too. The sooner we get to work the better."

Denise quickly pulled up two chairs.

"Paul," Captain Dubois said when they were all seated, "for several weeks now you've been reporting on the construction of this machine which the Nazis are putting up at Bruneval—the Fire Bowl. You probably didn't realize how valuable your work was. Neither did we. Nevertheless, all your reports were relayed to London, because we know the value of every little piece of information, no matter how unimportant it seems to be at the time.

"Up to now we've assumed that the Fire Bowl was some kind of super-searchlight, or possibly a large sound-detecting device like those which our own country used in the past—and which proved useless under modern conditions. Apparently it's neither of these things. Even now, none of us knows precisely what it is. In the past twenty-four hours the Allies have received new information about it, and they're very alarmed. They want every detail about it that we can supply, and that's why I asked you to come here. For example, three weeks ago you reported the arrival of several trucks carrying steel boxes and machinery. Now, think carefully. Can you remember any detail that might give us a clue as to where these trucks came from?"

Paul concentrated hard. Then he said ruefully, "No, Captain. I'm afraid I can only remember that they were ordinary German army trucks. There was no other identification on them."

"That's usually the case," Captain Dubois said. "But never mind. You see, if we knew where the trucks were loaded we might be able to trace what kind of apparatus they were carrying, where it was manufactured, and so on. The Allies could then bomb those factories if necessary, or we could try to sabotage them. Where were the boxes taken, Paul?"

"Into the house on the cliffs, sir. But later some of them were carried out to the pit in which the Fire Bowl stands."

"Good. So there is some kind of apparatus under the Fire Bowl itself?"

"Yes, Captain."

"Would you say it was complicated radio apparatus? More complicated than these radios we have here?"

"Oh, yes. There were big steel tables and lots of big meters. Most of the things I'd never seen before. It must have been very delicate, too, because the officers stood over the soldiers who were carrying it, shouting at them to be careful."

"I see. And in the Bowl itself, you're sure there isn't a lamp, or anything of that kind?"

"No. There isn't a lamp. There's just a little metal bar. I've never seen any light come out of the Bowl."

"How long is this bar?"

"I couldn't tell you exactly, sir. I've never been able to get close enough."

"Naturally. The important thing is that there isn't a lamp as would be the case with a searchlight, but a bar that doesn't light up.

Now, let's go on. Yesterday morning you were at the site of construction when a Spitfire flew over. Your cousin Theo told us about it. I want you to think carefully because this is vital. At the time the Spitfire flew over were you able to see what happened to the Fire Bowl?"

"It turned," Paul said slowly. "It turned, following the flight of the Spitfire. I saw that distinctly."

Captain Dubois jumped up. "Philippe!" he said to the man at the radio table. "Pass this on immediately. *We confirm that the Fire Bowl turned when the Spitfire flew over.*" He beamed down at Paul. "That's wonderful! Wonderful! You were on the spot to see the most vital thing of all!"

"Lamplighter here," the radio operator said quietly into a microphone. "Lamplighter here." He waited a moment, and Paul heard a slight grating sound come from his headphones. Then he said, "Lamplighter to London: the carrot twisted. Repeat: *twisted.*"

The grating sound came from his headphones again, and he began to scribble on his writing pad. "Message received," he said, and pressed a switch. He turned to the captain and passed him the sheet of writing.

The captain read it, and looked at Denise, then at Paul. "London asks us to stand by," he said. "They are deciding what action should be taken." He looked at his wrist watch and added, "It's now eight o'clock. We shall hear from them at ten. We have two hours to wait."

Half an hour later, at exactly eight-thirty, five men sat down at a conference table in London. Only one wore civilian clothes. The other four were high-ranking officers—one from the Royal Navy, one from the Army, and the other two from the Royal Air Force. Neatly arranged in front of each were writing pads, a stereoscope, and copies of the photographs, numbers 68 and 69, which had been taken over Bruneval the previous morning.

One of the R.A.F. officers opened the conference. He was Air Commodore Simpson.

In grave tones he said, "Gentlemen, this meeting has been called to discuss the two photographs lying before you. They were taken yesterday by a reconnaissance Spitfire flying over Northern France. I should be grateful if you would spend a few moments examining them through your stereoscopes. When you have done so, I will ask Professor Cheswick to explain what they mean, in terms of our present and future war strategy."

For several moments there was silence. Then the air commodore said, "Thank you. Now I'll call on Professor Cheswick who is, as you all know, one of the Prime Minister's scientific advisers."

Professor Cheswick rose, a tall elderly man with rather rumpled gray hair. He said: "Gentlemen, I'm afraid you haven't had much time to study these photographs; but I, and some of my colleagues, have been working on them most of the night. However, before I begin to tell you what I think they mean I should like to give you some background material, to explain why we feel they are so important.

"As you all know, after the fall of France in 1940 the Nazis began to attack Britain. They planned to weaken us by heavy bombing, and then to invade. They started by sending over large numbers of planes in daylight, but this wasn't very successful because the R.A.F. inflicted such terrible losses on them that they had to stop daylight raids.

"Then they began bombing at night. For some time this was successful. They did serious damage to London and many other cities.

"Now, the reason they were successful with their night bombing was simply because it's very difficult to find a plane in the sky at night. The sky is a big place. Human eyes don't see very well in the dark. And searchlights aren't very efficient at high altitudes. It's rather like trying to find a black pin in a pitch-black haystack.

"But recently you may have noticed that fewer Nazi bombers are reaching our big cities and that we've been shooting down more and more of them before they've had a chance to drop their bombs. The reason for this is that

we have perfected a device for detecting planes at night, or even in a fog or flying through dense cloud. This device is known as radio-location, or radar for short—standing for radio detection and ranging.

"Radar is without any question the most important scientific development of this war. Up to this time it has been the most closely guarded of all our secrets. It has been kept so secret that nobody knows about it except the

officers who are directly concerned with the installations, and, of course, those scientists who have been working on it.

"We knew that the Germans would try to find out why they have been losing so many planes at night. So a short while ago we planned a campaign to satisfy their curiosity. We let stories leak out that our pilots were being fed large quantities of carrots, which contain a substance called carotin. This carotin, we said, so improved the pilots' night vision that they were easily able to find the Nazi bombers in the dark.

"This campaign may have impressed Hitler, and he may have ordered his pilots to eat lots of carrots, too. But the Germans have some very clever scientists. I don't think they would have been fooled for long by this carrot story. Sooner or later they were bound to develop radar for themselves. We were ahead of them for a good long time—long enough to save Britain from destruction and defeat after Dunkirk. But the evidence now goes to show that they, too, have developed radar. To the best of my knowledge, these photographs show a radar station in operation at Bruneval, in Northern France. A few minutes ago we received a message from the Resistance that tends to confirm this."

There was a long silence.

Then the naval officer asked, "Professor Cheswick: is this device only used for detecting planes flying at night?"

"No, sir," the scientist answered. "It will

detect and pin-point ships as far as twenty miles away, giving you such accuracy that you can lay your guns and destroy them before they've even become aware that you are anywhere near them. In modified form, it will even detect submarines lying on the sea bottom."

"That means," the naval officer said calmly, "that if we are planning an invasion of Europe we have to take into account the fact that the Nazis could detect our invasion fleet even in the darkness?"

"Yes." The reply came bluntly.

The army officer said, "It looks, therefore, as if we'll have to change our plans for the invasion completely."

Air Commodore Simpson said, "We're going to have to change our plans for bombing Germany, too. This is a completely new factor, which is going to change all our strategy."

"Do we have any details of this radar station of Bruneval?" the naval officer asked. "I mean, its power, its range, and so on?"

"Very little," Professor Cheswick said.

"The first thing we really have to find out is precisely this—what it can do. It may be much better than our radar. On the other hand, it may be less efficient. Until we know for sure how far the Germans have developed their radar system it's impossible for us to make any plans at all. When we *do* find out, we can make our plans accordingly."

"How do you propose to find out, Professor?" the army officer asked.

The air commodore intervened. "At the present moment," he said, "a young Frenchman named Paul Martin is at Resistance headquarters somewhere in Normandy. Paul Martin has done a remarkable job—he watched and reported the building of this station at Bruneval. He knows more about it than anybody on the Allied side. We're in radio contact with this headquarters—which goes under the code name of Lamplighter— and they are standing by for a message from us at ten o'clock. The suggestion I want to make is that we should talk to young Paul Martin as soon as possible."

"By short-wave radio?" the naval officer asked.

"That," Air Commodore Simpson said grimly, "is something we can now discuss."

At ten o'clock, to the second, the radio operator's earphones began to crackle. He glanced round at Captain Dubois and said warningly, "London calling."

Paul, Denise and the captain were crowding round his table. Philippe, the operator, began to take down a message, writing swiftly on his pad. When it was finished he said, "Yes, London. Lamplighter will stand by," and turned to the captain, a strange look in his eye. "London is waiting," he said. "They ask for an immediate answer."

Captain Dubois picked up the writing pad and read the message slowly. Then he said in a tense, quiet voice, "Paul, the Allies must have everything you know about the Fire Bowl. They want to question you in detail, but it is difficult to do this by radio. They want to send a motor torpedo boat to pick you up at midnight and take you to England. It is for you, and only you, to decide whether you will go. What do you say?"

Paul stared at him. "They want me to go to England?"

"Yes. But you must realize that it is a dangerous journey. Anything could happen."

Paul looked at Denise, then at the captain. He smiled. "But of course I'll go," he said. "I'll be proud to go."

Denise laughed with joy. Captain Dubois whirled around to Philippe. "Give them that for their answer," he cried. "Radio this: Lamplighter to London. Resistance man Paul Martin will be proud to go. The appointment will be kept at midnight."

CHAPTER 5

E-Boat!

FOR TWO HOURS the old fishing trawler *Dauphin* had dipped and rolled in the dirty waters of the English Channel. Her engines chugged away sluggishly, missing every now and then, and they did not appear to have sufficient power to drive her through the heavy seas. The result was that she was drifting further and further away from her home port, and the tide was carrying her slowly and surely toward a point some four miles off the beautiful village of Etretat.

Her decks were littered with fishing gear. Her crew, which included Paul Martin and Captain Dubois, looked thoroughly disreputable. They were all dirty and disheveled; their oilskins were streaming from the seas the boat shipped every few minutes. Occasionally, when the engines spat and misfired, the *Dauphin* sat back in the waves like a stubborn mule, losing all her leeway, looking for all the world as if she were refusing to go another inch. Anybody who could have seen the old tub wallowing in the darkness would have realized that she was in trouble. The old wreck was surely on her last legs.

But she continued to drift toward Etretat. Steadily and surely she continued to drift toward her meeting with a certain British motor torpedo boat.

In the stern of the boat Captain Dubois said to Paul, "It's amazing, isn't it, that a small piece of cotton waste in the fuel line can cause so much trouble!"

Paul, who was still in a daze from all the happenings of the past twenty-four hours, said hesitantly, "Does the skipper of the *Dauphin* know about this?"

"The mate put it there on the skipper's instructions," Captain Dubois said, laughing. "It can be removed in a couple of minutes. But, you see, we aren't allowed in these waters. If by bad luck we should be caught by an E-boat we might have serious difficulty explaining what we're doing here. As it is—" He shrugged his shoulders eloquently. "Our engines are disabled. Can we help it if our boat is drifting?"

"Captain, are we getting near the place where we're supposed to meet the British motor torpedo boat?" Paul asked. It was hard for him to control his voice, hard to control his anxiety that somehow the *Dauphin* would fail to meet the British boat.

"I've just spoken to the skipper," Captain Dubois said reassuringly. "We're almost there. You can trust him, Paul. He hasn't failed us yet."

In the wheelhouse the skipper stood looking out into the darkness, his strong old hands
correcting the *Dauphin's* drift with absolute
sureness. He had been sailing in these waters
since he was a boy of twelve—for fifty long
years. He knew how calm they could be, and
how fierce and treacherous; he had fought for
his life on them and slept peacefully on them,
and they had been the scene he had spent most
of his life watching. If all went well he would
bring the *Dauphin* to her rendezvous within
fifteen minutes, and safely transfer to the British MTB this young Frenchman they were so
anxious to have in London. But he knew the
chances were very great that sometime on this
trip he would be challenged by one of the
German boats that swarmed off this coast. He
could only hope that if luck were against him
it would happen after Paul had been trans-
ferred. Otherwise . . . well, it might be too
bad. In the meantime, he was matching his
cunning against the Nazis' ferocity. He carried no guns. Only brains, and the wisdom of
fifty years on this wild sea.

The *Dauphin* drifted on. When the tide carried her too far off course, he signaled to the mate for a short burst of power to bring her back under control. The minutes ticked on, marked only by the relentless pounding of the waves. It was ten minutes to zero hour. He could imagine the MTB coming closer and closer, a great shower of spray curving up from her bows, her motors roaring—

Was that the British boat? He thought he could hear the sound of motors coming toward him. But it was too early, and the rendezvous was still a mile away. The British were good seamen; they were always on time to the second, always.

A searchlight wavered in the darkness, caught the *Dauphin*, grew brighter and more frightening. A shell screamed over the mast of the old trawler. "E-boat," the skipper called down from the wheelhouse, and Paul became rigid at Captain Dubois' side.

"Don't be scared," the captain said calmly. "Nothing serious is going to happen. They'll just look us over and go away."

The E-boat, low and powerful, came throbbing alongside. Small, tremendously fast, these craft carried guns and torpedoes, harrying Allied shipping in the English Channel and controlling the French ports. They were even faster than the British motor torpedo boats, but they were more vulnerable because of their lighter construction.

A harsh voice called over a loud-hailer, "Heave to, there. What ship are you?"

The skipper shouted back through a battered megaphone, "The French fishing trawler *Dauphin*."

The harsh voice shook with rage. "You know that you are forbidden in these waters. What are you doing out here?"

"Our engines have broken down. We are drifting. I am trying to return to Etretat on the incoming tide."

The loud-hailer sputtered with fury. "You are lying. You are here in defiance of regulations."

"Herr Commander," the skipper called back. "At the rate we are drifting we cannot get back to port until morning. I would be obliged if you would tow me. Permit me to throw you a line—"

It was a sly move on his part. The last thing the commander of the E-boat would do would be to divert his vessel from its patrol duty in order to tow a lumbering old fishing trawler through heavy seas.

"Don't lie to me!" the voice bellowed. "Assemble your crew on the starboard bow."

The skipper called down, "You heard what the Herr Commander said. Line up on the starboard bow." He added, for the benefit of the crew, "But take your time. There's no hurry, lads."

Paul asked Captain Dubois in a low voice, "What should I do now?"

"Line up with the rest of us," the captain answered. "They won't recognize you—you look like a dashing young sailor. And don't worry. The skipper will see us through this affair."

He sauntered up to the rail, into the blinding glare of the searchlight; Paul followed him. Beside Paul stood the mate in a dirty T-shirt, his arms covered with thick black oil, a huge spanner in one hand. He was snarling and muttering under his breath. With him were three other members of the crew, dirty, wet, unshaven, shuffling their feet.

The searchlight swung along the bedraggled line. Paul could see nothing in the blaze of light, but he knew that the E-boat's guns were manned and trained on the *Dauphin*.

One command would be enough to blow the *Dauphin* to fragments.

"Take off your hats," the voice shouted through the loud-hailer.

Slowly, bitterly, each man removed his sou'wester. It was an order given to enable the Nazis to get a better look at the men's faces, but they took it as an indignity, resenting it and hating the enemy who gave it.

Slowly the searchlight moved back and forth, like a blazing white eye from which there was no escape. It hovered on each man in turn, and Paul stiffened as it reached him and gave a deep inward sigh as it passed on to the mate.

A shattering roar came from the loud-hailer. "That boy! *Who is that boy?*"

The searchlight swung back, seemed to leap at Paul and fasten itself upon him. He froze. He felt exactly as if the Nazi commander had leaned forward and pointed a finger at him, as if the machine guns on the E-boat's deck were now aimed directly at his body.

"He's my nephew," the skipper shouted

back through the megaphone. "I'm short of men and I had to bring him out with me."

The harsh voice ignored the skipper's explanation. "Schultz! Figl! Prepare to board this boat! Examine her papers and question the boy! Proceed at once!"

A rope came flying from the E-boat onto the *Dauphin's* deck. For one heavy moment every Frenchman turned to stare at it sullenly, but nobody moved. Another order roared out of the loud-hailer. "Make fast, there! If you fail to obey you will be responsible for the consequences."

"Make fast," the skipper called from the wheelhouse; and the mate left the rail, looped the rope around a capstan, and stood glowering, awaiting the next command. There was no alternative. The unarmed fishing trawler was completely at the mercy of the E-boat.

Black and throbbing, like a giant whale shark, the E-boat drew close. The decks of both craft were almost level, and suddenly they seemed to lock together in the trough of a wave. A Nazi sailor with a sub-machine gun slung over his back, leaped onto the *Dauphin*. But there was no chance for the second man to follow him. A hoarse cry of panic came from the E-boat's loud-hailer, *"Achtung! Achtung!"* with a string of furious orders. Paul, wondering what had happened, became aware in that moment of a rumble of sound on the *Dauphin's* port bow, growing louder and louder like the rolling of drums.

The E-boat's engines crackled savagely, and Paul saw the sea boil into foam as she hastily backed away from the *Dauphin*. The rope linking the two boats tightened, then slackened as somebody on the E-boat cast it off. The searchlight snapped out, and the world became black again and filled with terrifying noise as the E-boat opened up in an attempt to reach full speed and race away.

"The British motor torpedo boat!" Captain Dubois cried exultantly. "She must have seen us in the E-boat's searchlight!"

The Nazi sailor on the deck of the *Dauphin* stood in utter bewilderment, staring into the darkness, listening to the E-boat shrieking away. He did not realize his peril. In one cat-like leap the mate reached him, struck at the angle of neck and shoulder blade and sent him sprawling into a pile of fish net. Two of the crew pounced on him and tied his arms and legs before he could even give a moan.

"Clear the engines!" the skipper called from the wheelhouse. "This may get too hot for us. We'd better start moving."

A star shell went curving up into the sky and burst with a hot blue-white flare that hung in the black emptiness before it began to fall slowly. Which boat had fired it Paul could not tell; but, crowding into the bows with the rest of the crew, he saw the low hull of the MTB streaking through the waves toward the *Dauphin*. The E-boat, a few hundred yards away, was almost hidden in its own wake as it built up speed. He heard the sharp crack of guns, and then a shout from the skipper, "The Nazi is coming back! Down on your faces, every one of you!"

The E-boat had turned like a jack rabbit, heading back for the trawler, its engines making a noise like calico being ripped apart. It passed close to the *Dauphin,* its machine guns rattling vindictively, as if the Nazi commander had decided that the *Dauphin* had acted as a decoy, luring him into this battle with the MTB. Paul heard the bullets whistle over-head, and waited a moment before he raised his head to see what was happening now. The British boat was rocketing past in full pursuit. As it passed, another star shell flooded the sky with light and showed the E-boat zigzagging away, twisting and rolling. Suddenly, once more, she came leaping back for another stab at the *Dauphin;* but this time the *Dauphin* replied in kind. Captain Dubois had snatched up the sub-machine gun which had fallen from the Nazi's body, and was firing back furi-ously. The E-boat veered off. Then Paul saw a thickening white line of bubbles traveling fast toward the trawler, and his heart almost stopped beating.

"Torpedo!" the skipper bawled.

The *Dauphin* juddered as its engines burst into life, and the old boat heeled over as the

skipper applied full rudder. The line of bubbles streamed past the *Dauphin's* stern and
went steadily on into the darkness of the sea.
Paul breathed again.

It seemed like hours, but the fight had
lasted only a few minutes. The E-boat had
been caught flat-footed. Before it could build
up full speed, the British boat had pounced
upon it, pouring a devastating hail of shells
and bullets into its fragile hull. It made a last
desperate effort to reach the *Dauphin,* but a
hundred yards away it seemed to stop in its
tracks, the sleek powerful body gave a great
shudder and then flew apart in a mighty sheet
of flame. The blast shot across the heaving
water, and Paul felt the hot air slap at his face,
and ducked. The E-boat's main magazine
must have been hit; and every man on board
her must have died in that single moment of
history.

There was no time now for delay. The brief
battle might have alerted other E-boats, and
a swarm of them might be converging on this

spot at full speed. The floating fragments of wreckage might give them all the evidence they needed to begin a desperate hunt for the MTB, and the sooner it turned back for home the better for all concerned.

It wheeled around and bore down on the *Dauphin* in a shower of spray. Once again the giant voice of a loud-hailer crackled. "Ahoy, there! What ship are you?"

"The *Dauphin*."

"Good. Prepare to transfer your passenger."

"We have an extra passenger—one of the crew of the E-boat."

"We'll take him, too. The more the merrier. Transfer your Nazi first."

In the short time that remained on board the *Dauphin* Captain Dubois took Paul's hand and said warmly, "Au revoir, Paul. I look forward to seeing you again soon. Remember, the Resistance is proud of you. You have done a man's work for us."

Paul choked slightly. "Thank you, Captain."

"I would like to give you some advice be-

fore we part. First: do not return to France
too soon. The Nazis have long memories; they
will continue to look for you. Second, how old
are you?"

"Fifteen," Paul replied.

Captain Dubois chuckled. "You have my
permission to tell our Allies that you are
eighteen. Otherwise you will miss a lot of
fun."

"Yes, sir," Paul said, but this second piece
of advice puzzled him.

"Paul Martin!" came a cry from the bow.

"Ready!" Paul called back, and as he turned
to leave he felt a reassuring touch on his
shoulder.

"Good luck," Captain Dubois said. "And
good hunting."

CHAPTER 6

A Very Important Person

PAUL sat on the edge of a narrow bunk drinking a mug of hot cocoa. A thick blanket was draped around him, but even so he was shivering with cold. He was in a tiny cabin under the control bridge of the motor torpedo boat, and a tall young lieutenant wearing a thick sheepskin jacket was watching him with twinkling eyes, smiling down in a friendly way.

86

"So you're the Very Important Person we had to come all this distance to pick up," the lieutenant said. He was a Canadian, and he spoke French fluently but with an accent that sounded rather strange to Paul. "And how old are you, young man?"

Paul remembered Captain Dubois' parting advice. "Eighteen," he answered, keeping his eyes lowered.

"Eighteen, eh?" the lieutenant laughed. "Well, when you've finished your cocoa I suggest you pull that nice woolly blanket over your head and get some sleep. You've had quite a night, and I guess you're going to have an even busier time when you get to London."

"Sleep!" Paul protested. "Oh, no!" The suggestion shocked him. *Sleep,* on his first trip in a motor torpedo boat! *Sleep,* the first time he was with the Allies who were going to liberate France! Impossible!

"All right," the lieutenant said. "I'll just go and have a few words with our Nazi passenger, and then if you like I'll come back and show you what makes a motor torpedo boat tick. In the meantime, sit there and make yourself comfortable."

Paul smiled at him gratefully, and sat back listening to the deep roar of the engines, the shrill sounds outside as the boat cut through the waves. He could feel it lurching and twisting like an eel, and sometimes it seemed to leap clean out of the water. He wondered what his sensations would be if he could hold the controls of this power-packed little fighting ship for a minute or two, and his eyes closed happily as he imagined himself on the control bridge. He was looking ahead over the boiling spray thrown up by the bows. The roar of the engines was growing louder and louder as he squeezed the last ounce of speed out of them. The MTB was a living thing of muscle and sinew leaping ahead like a panther . . .

The lieutenant was shaking him gently. He opened his eyes in confusion, thinking vaguely, *I must have dozed off;* but to his surprise the tall lieutenant said with a grin, "We're just coming into port, young man. You'd better get ready to go ashore." Still heavy with sleep, Paul followed him up onto the crowded deck. When his eyes had become accustomed to the darkness he saw that they were in a large harbor, passing the black silent shapes of scores of warships that all towered over the motor torpedo boat. Pin points of light blinked inquisitively, challenging the MTB's identity; a sailor on the bridge replied with an Aldis lamp, opening and closing the shutter to give the answering signals.

The boat slipped quietly to a jetty, slowed, came to rest. Then, almost before he knew what was happening, Paul was on land again, his legs wavering, his head spinning. The solid feel of concrete made him strangely dizzy after so many hours at sea.

"Come along with me, Paul," the lieutenant said, and began to walk rapidly toward some dark buildings at the far end of the jetty. But Paul had difficulty keeping up with him. The concrete seemed to wobble like jelly under his feet.

The lieutenant laughed pleasantly. "Don't worry," he said. "You'll find your land legs in a couple of minutes," and he put his hand on Paul's shoulder to steady him.

An armed sentry, with rifle leveled, stepped out of the darkness suddenly with a sharp order, "Halt and be recognized!" The lieutenant identified himself, and the sentry saluted and stepped back to continue his lonely watch. Twenty yards away another sentry stopped them. There were two more on guard at the

entrance to the building into which the lieutenant led Paul. This was his first impression
of wartime Britain—a dark fortress, guarded
by grim sentries at every turn.

He was taken into a small bare room where
a naval officer sat at a table going through a
large stack of papers, and the lieutenant said
briskly, "Sorry to be late, sir. But here's your
Very Important Person, Paul Martin."

The officer rose. Paul saw that he was tall
and thin, rather like Theo; and, like Theo, he
moved with some difficulty because of a stiff
leg.

He said to the lieutenant, "Did you run into
any trouble?"

"An E-boat," the lieutenant said. He
grinned. "We arrived at the scene of the crime
just as it was having an argument with the
Dauphin. It had actually put an armed guard
on board the *Dauphin,* and we brought the
fellow back with us. That's the score for today: one E-boat sunk, one prisoner named
Schultz, and one V.I.P. named Paul Martin."

"Really?" the other man said. He looked

thoughtful for a moment, said politely to Paul, "Sit down, please," and stepped aside to talk to the lieutenant in a low voice. The conversation lasted for several minutes, and then the lieutenant left with a cheerful farewell to Paul.

The tall elderly officer limped back to the table and said, "Now, then. We can settle down to our business. Let me introduce myself, by the way. I'm Commander Lake." He held his hand out, and Paul rose courteously to shake it.

"You had quite an adventurous trip, I hear," the commander said as he sat down. "Were you scared when you were stopped by the E-boat?"

"A little," Paul admitted. "I was afraid I wouldn't get here. And it isn't a nice experience to be captured by the Nazis."

"So I imagine," Commander Lake said. "Tell me about the E-boat. Have you ever seen one before?"

"No, sir."

"No? I thought you lived by the sea? E-boats pass up and down the coast all the time, don't they?"

"I've seen them in the distance, sir. But the Nazis don't allow us to go on the cliffs or near the harbors. They've put barbed wire and guards everywhere. The farm is as far as I've been allowed to go."

"The farm?"

"Yes. It's called Le Presbytère. The priest lived there once, but no longer. And even the farmer doesn't live there now. The Nazis have taken it over."

"I see. And you have no idea where the E-boat came from?"

"No, sir," Paul answered. The questions puzzled him.

"Do you have any idea how the E-boat happened to discover the *Dauphin?*"

"No, sir." Paul thought for a moment. "But it was something that Captain Dubois feared. It's very difficult to evade the E-boats along that stretch of coast."

"Who is Captain Dubois?"

"He's one of the leaders of the Resistance, sir."

Commander Lake nodded and took a sheet of paper out of a drawer in his desk. "Now," he said, "I should like to ask you a few personal questions, just for our records. Your full name?"

"Paul Martin."

The commander wrote it down. "Your age?"

Again Paul recollected Captain Dubois' advice. "Eighteen."

The commander glanced at him in surprise but made no comment. "Where do you live?"

"Bruneval."

On and on the questions went. Finally Commander Lake put his pen down, leaned back in his chair and said, "Paul, do you know why you've been brought here?"

"Yes, sir. Because of the Fire Bowl."

"The Fire Bowl?"

Paul smiled. "It has another name. *Carrots*."

Commander Lake said, "Thank you, Paul. That's all I want to know for the time being. At six o'clock this morning you will be driven up to London." He looked at his watch. "That gives you time to snatch about two and a half hours' sleep. Are you hungry? Would you like to eat something before you rest?"

"I'm not hungry, sir," Paul said. "I'm not really tired, either. This is all so exciting!"

"Even though you're all of eighteen," the commander said with a little laugh, "you still need to get a little sleep now and then." He picked up his telephone and spoke into it briefly. A minute later there was a sharp knock at the door and two marines entered at Commander Lake's call of "Come in." They were tall powerful men, armed with revolvers.

"Until you leave here," Commander Lake said, "you will be in the care of these guards, Paul. You're the most important young man in England at present and we have to take good care of you."

"Yes, sir," Paul said. He looked up at the two marines in awe.

"Don't be scared of them," the commander said, a gleam of amusement in his eyes. "They're actually as gentle as kittens." He addressed the marines. "This lad can bed down in my bunk until he's ready to leave. A car will be at the front gate at 0630 hours to take him to London. Make sure that he doesn't miss it."

"Yes, sir."

"He will be accompanied on that trip by a Sergeant Villard, whose credentials you will personally inspect before he's allowed to leave with this boy."

"Very good, sir."

"That's all," Commander Lake said, and he watched the two powerful men lead Paul out of the room. Then he pulled a fresh sheet of paper out of his drawer and wrote on it:

SUBJECT: PAUL MARTIN
Subject answered all questions
satisfactorily (see attached
sheet) with exception of his age,
which seems rather exaggerated. He
is willing and intelligent. How-

```
ever, the circumstances of the
Dauphin's meeting with the E-boat
lend themselves to suspicion, and
I recommend that the subject be
investigated further before he is
taken into full confidence with
regard to our plans for Carrots.
```

                    (Signed)

                        B. E. Lake
                        Commander, R.N.

The voice that wakened Paul a few hours later was gay and teasing, a voice that might have come from his own village.

"Come on, my boy! Up! Up! A beautiful new day is beginning! Open your eyes and enjoy it!"

Paul opened his eyes and gave a little groan. For a moment he had no idea where he was. A man he had never seen before was standing over him, wearing a blue uniform and a neat pointed cap. The room was filled with unfamiliar objects—books, a phonograph, photographs of strangers, paintings of ships. The last place in which he had slept was the cabin of the MTB. Before that, in the caves of Bruneval. Now, here . . . It was all too confusing.

"Who are you?" he said sleepily to the man.

"Gaston Villard, sergeant in the Free French Air Force. At your service, my bleary-eyed young countryman. Now, will you get up of your own free will, or must I pour a jug of cold water over your head?"

"The Free French Air Force!" Paul cried in wonder. His eyes shone with pleasure. This, like the Resistance, was one of the legends of France—a company of dauntless men who had eluded the Nazis, escaped to England, and, flying Allied planes, had astonished the whole world by their gallantry. The heart of any Frenchman would have grown big with pride at meeting one of these men. And the least Paul could do was to scramble out of his warm, comfortable bed immediately.

"Ah!" Gaston said, beaming. "That's better! Now I can tell that you have been well brought up."

He was not very tall, but it was easy to see

that he was strong. His shoulders were broad, his hips narrow. He had deep brown eyes and such a tough beard that his chin was nearly as blue as his uniform. While Paul washed and dressed, Gaston kept up a steady flow of conversation. "Yes. I am from Normandy, too, my young cockerel. From Bayeux. You have been there? No? You *haven't*? But that's terrible, my friend, terrible. I can't understand how your education has been so neglected. I will

take you there personally, when we have set-
tled the hash of these Nazis. You have heard
of the cathedral, of course? And the great tap-
estry woven by Queen Mathilde? Yes. And the
food? The butter, eggs, cheese, pastries? Oh,
my mouth waters when I think of them.
Hurry, my boy, and we may have time for a
morsel of breakfast before we leave here.
Hurry! I am so hungry I could eat a horse.
Tail and all."

Breathlessly, Paul pulled on his clothes.

Gaston looked at him and wrinkled his delicate nose. "What are these things you are
wearing? An old jersey, dirty old pants, boots
that are six sizes too large for you? What goes
on here? Is this the way young Frenchmen
dress these days? But you have to meet many
important people. You should look neat and
tidy, a credit to French taste and breeding."

"It's a kind of disguise," Paul explained
apologetically. "You see, I was on a fishing
trawler, and there was a possibility that we
might be captured by the Nazis, so I had to
wear these old clothes. It would have looked

strange if I'd worn anything else. I had to look like a fisherman. It was Captain Dubois' idea."

"Captain Dubois?" Gaston asked. "Who is he?"

"A leader of the Resistance in Normandy."

"Of course!" Gaston exclaimed. "I know him well. He's a great friend of mine. A big chap, with only one eye . . ."

"No," Paul said. "The Captain Dubois I mean hasn't lost an eye."

"You're sure?"

"Absolutely," Paul said. "We were together all yesterday and last night."

"Where? At his headquarters?"

"Yes."

"I've been to his headquarters, at least. They are in the cellar of a château—"

"No. In a home for old ladies."

"Is that so? Well, perhaps I'm thinking of somebody else. Doesn't he have a girl working for him? Let me see. What's her name? Marie?"

"Denise," Paul said.

"Yes. That's right. Now, are you dressed? Then let's go. A bite of breakfast, and after that a nice long ride through the countryside."

Paul didn't move.

"Come on!" Gaston said. "What are you waiting for?"

"All these questions," Paul said. "All these questions. You're trying to trap me in some way."

"You think I am?" Gaston said, raising his eyebrows.

"Yes. And when I arrived here, Commander Lake asked me a lot of questions like that, too. What's the matter? Don't you believe I'm honest? Do you think I've come here to tell you all a lot of lies?"

Gaston's face became grave. "Paul, I want to warn you now. This is only the beginning. You will be asked a lot of questions, and many people will try to trap you. It's wartime, and we have to be on our guard. The reason you were brought here is so important and secret that we cannot take any chances. Even I, Gaston Villard, do not know what it is. But before we can trust you we have to know for certain that you are, beyond any doubt, Paul Martin from Bruneval. How can we be sure, if we don't ask questions, that you aren't a spy whom the Germans substituted for the real Paul Martin?"

"Oh, no!" Paul cried. "Oh, no!"

"If you answer the questions," Gaston said quietly, "you have nothing to fear. But, at the same time, my innocent young friend, be careful what you say and to whom you say it. For example, you have told me the name of the leader of the Resistance in Normandy, the name of the girl who works with him, and where they work. How do you know that I'm not a spy myself, who somehow managed to get in here? I might walk out of this room and radio the information you gave me to the German military authorities. That would be the end of Captain Dubois and Denise."

"But you told me you're in the Free French Air Force—"

"And you told Commander Lake that

you're Paul Martin, from the Resistance,"
Gaston replied.

Paul darkened with anger. Then suddenly
he smiled. "Yes," he said, "I understand."

"From now on," Gaston said, "remember
one thing—guard your tongue. Take the strict-
est care that the enemy doesn't surprise any
secrets out of you. As for myself, I'll set your
mind at rest," and he pulled a leather wallet
out of his pocket and showed Paul a small
card.

It read:

FREE FRENCH AIR FORCE
GASTON VILLARD
SERGEANT: SECURITY POLICE

CHAPTER 7

A Meeting with the Allies

THE DRIVE to London took a little more than two and a half hours. A girl in a neat khaki uniform drove the big olive-drab car, handling it with quiet efficiency. Beside her sat an armed military policeman. Paul and Gaston occupied the back seat.

It was hardly believable to Paul that on these roads there was not a single Nazi patrol car, that in all this countryside there was not a single Nazi check-point. France, so near to England, separated by only a narrow strip of sea, was practically helpless. Hundreds of thousands of men in the uniform of the German Army had overrun the land, and the French people had virtually no means of resisting them. Here, the endless convoys of trucks that Paul saw rumbling along the roads all belonged to the Allies; every able-bodied man was in uniform—Allied uniform; the airplanes in the sky were all Allied planes. His heart filled with hope.

But the British people had not escaped the horrors of war. Even in the small villages through which the car passed there were piles of rubble that had once been houses. Even in the open country there were farm buildings that had been destroyed by fire and high explosives; even in the fields themselves there were huge bomb craters. The outskirts of London looked in places as if they had been stricken by a colossal earthquake. Entire blocks of buildings had crumbled into a wilderness of dust and shattered bricks. Paul saw houses that had been cut open from top to bottom, as if by a giant knife; houses that were merely blackened shells, burned out by incendiary bombs. The Nazis boasted that they had reduced London to ruins, but Paul had never believed this. Now, however, he saw some of the terrible wounds the city had received, and he marveled at the courage of the people who had survived the ordeal of bombs and fire night after night, and who were still fighting back with all their strength.

Gaston must have guessed Paul's thoughts. "You needn't fear," he said. "The Nazis are never going to destroy London. What's more, for every bomb they've dropped here there will be ten dropped on their own heads. They're going to learn the lesson that aggression doesn't pay; and I'm afraid they're going to learn it the hard way." He pointed through the window on Paul's side. "Look! Have you seen the barrage balloons?"

The sky seemed to be filled with them. They floated just beneath the clouds on immensely long cables; hundreds and hundreds of plump silvery balloons that looked like baby elephants.

"The Nazis are afraid to fly anywhere near them at night," Gaston explained. "The cables can cut off the wing of a plane as neatly as a knife cuts through butter. And it's impossible to predict where they're going to be. Sometimes they're hidden way up in the clouds; sometimes they're low." His eyes shone with enthusiasm. "Think of it, Paul! Only eighteen months ago the Germans were absolutely certain that they could bring this country to its knees by bombing. They tried bombing by day, and our Hurricanes and Spitfires slaughtered them. They tried bombing by night, and again we are beating them. In some miraculous way we can find them in the dark. Soon it will be suicide for any Nazi to fly over Allied territory, by day or by night."

The car crossed a wide bridge, and Paul saw the majestic buildings of the Houses of Parliament and the tall tower which housed Big Ben. He knew the deep noble chimes of that clock very well. They were broadcast on the radio every day and heard in attics and cellars all over Europe, where people secretly listened to the voice of freedom. The Nazis threatened death to anybody found listening to these broadcasts, but their most ferocious threats could not silence Big Ben. People still listened. The great chimes still rang out.

The car swung into a broad street. "Whitehall," Gaston said. "The nerve center of our armies, our navies, and our air power." He pointed to a tiny street, scarcely more than an alley, hemmed in by tall buildings. "And that's Downing Street, where Winston Churchill lives. His house is number ten; one of the most famous houses in the world."

The car turned and stopped. The military policeman jumped out and opened the door for Paul and Gaston.

"The Air Ministry," Gaston said. "This is where the fun really begins."

It was not really fun. Paul sat at a table with three men. One, in civilian clothes, was Professor Cheswick. The other two, in R.A.F.

uniforms, were Air Commodore Simpson and Squadron Leader Marshall, from Intelligence Headquarters.

Paul was quaking inwardly. They had been firing questions at him for hours, or so it seemed. And not about the Fire Bowl, but about himself, about his relatives and friends and the life he had led at Bruneval. *Your name . . . Your father's name . . . Your mother's, before she married . . . Your address . . . Where did you go to school? . . . Theo Leblanc's address . . . When did he come to live at your house? . . .*

As the questions continued, Paul became frightened. The three men were friendly and polite, but he had a feeling that they did not believe anything he said, that they did not even believe that he was really Paul Martin. He wanted to cry in despair, "*Why* don't you believe me?" but he controlled himself, remembering what Gaston had said early that morning, and answered all the questions in a firm, steady voice.

At last Squadron Leader Marshall placed in front of him two small square photographs and a curious instrument which he had never seen before. "This is a stereoscope," the squadron leader said. "Look through it, please. Take your time until it becomes clear and then tell us whether you see anything you recognize."

Paul stared through the lenses at the photographs. For a few seconds he saw only a blur. Then, in a miraculous way, the two photographs merged into one and he cried in astonishment, "Yes! There is the Fire Bowl! And there's the house on the cliffs. This is the Fire Bowl installation at Bruneval!"

He was filled with wonder. It was like looking down at the Fire Bowl from a tall building. Everything stood out in relief, and he felt that if he reached out his hand he could actually touch it.

Squadron Leader Marshall said, "Yes. Now, Paul, listen carefully. These photographs were taken by a Spitfire which flew over Bruneval early in the morning of the day before yesterday. Look at the pictures again, and tell us what you see in the top left-hand corner. And *think!*"

There was silence for nearly a minute, until Paul raised his eyes from the stereoscope. His heart was beating wildly. He looked at the squadron leader and said, "In the top left-hand corner, near the trees, there seems to be a small group of people. If I had a stronger magnifiying glass I might be able to tell you for certain; I was near this spot when the Spitfire flew over the other morning. Three German soldiers had captured me. They threw themselves on the ground, and I was able to escape when the plane flew out to sea. Perhaps I'm wrong—"

"No," Air Commodore Simpson said with a smile. "You aren't wrong. We've checked very carefully, and you were near the installation at the precise moment the Spitfire took these photographs." He turned to the other two men. "I think this young man has established his identity beyond any reasonable doubt. Do you agree?"

They nodded.

The air commodore turned back to Paul. "I'm sorry that you were made to undergo such long questioning," he said quietly. "Not only from us, but from Commander Lake and Sergeant Villard who accompanied you here. I think you'll understand, though, that we had to check all the facts very carefully. We had to be extra-cautious after we heard that an E-boat was alongside the *Dauphin* last night before you were taken off. We had to make sure the Nazis hadn't sent us a young man in your place. They're very clever people, these Nazis, and they've done such a thing more than once before."

He paused. Then he went on, "In a way, Paul, all this questioning may have a good result. You must have realized by now that we sent for you because of something vitally important to the Allied cause; so important that we dare not take any chances concerning it. Furthermore, it is all absolutely secret. You mustn't speak to anybody about the Fire Bowl, except with our permission. You mustn't tell anybody that we brought you over here specially, because it will be easy to associate you with Bruneval, and thus with the Fire Bowl. Do you understand?"

"Yes, sir," Paul answered firmly.

"Good. Now, if you please, I want you to wait in the next room for a few moments."

Paul stood up and walked to the next room,

where Gaston was waiting. When the door closed, Air Commodore Simpson said to Professor Cheswick, "Well, what do you think of our young Frenchman?"

Professor Cheswick answered slowly, "I think we can consider ourselves very fortunate. For a boy of his age he's exceptionally quick and intelligent. I'm sure he'll be of great assistance to us."

"Squadron leader?" the air commodore asked.

"I agree," Squadron Leader Marshall said. "And he's not only quick and intelligent; he's plucky. He stood up to all the questions we asked him without batting an eyelid. There's only one thing I'm doubtful about. How old is he exactly?"

The air commodore laughed. "There seems to be some dispute about that. I understood at first that he was fifteen. Now he claims to be eighteen."

"Why should he falsify his age?" Professor Cheswick asked.

"I can only make a guess," Air Commodore

Simpson replied. "At fifteen he would be considered still a boy. At eighteen he's a man, old enough for any military duty. It's another good mark to his credit; he doesn't want to miss any of the excitement that goes on around here. Professor, I feel we can add him to our team without any further hullabaloo. Will you now take charge of him and see that he gets to work on the Bruneval problem?"

"Yes," the professor said.

"Good. Incidentally, have you had any reaction from the Prime Minister on this Bruneval business?"

Professor Cheswick glanced at his watch. "The Prime Minister is holding a meeting in three-quarters of an hour to discuss it. I hope we'll get a firm decision then."

"I hope and pray that he realizes the full importance of Bruneval," Air Commodore Simpson said earnestly.

"I'm sure he does," the professor said. "I shall be present at the meeting, and I intend to take good care that everybody else realizes its full importance, too. In the meantime, squadron leader, I should be glad if you would look after Paul until the meeting is over. I'd like to take him over to Intelligence Headquarters this afternoon so that we can start work at once."

"Yes, sir," Squadron Leader Marshall said. "And what about the sergeant who brought him here? Shall I tell him to return to his unit?"

The professor's keen eyes narrowed. "The sergeant is a Frenchman too, isn't he?"

"Yes, sir. In the Free French Air Force. With a very fine record."

"Then keep him! Keep him!" the professor cried. "I tell you, before this thing is over we shall need every good man we can find. Keep him!"

In the Cabinet Room of 10 Downing Street, some three-quarters of an hour later, the Prime Minister of Great Britain listened grimly to Professor Cheswick's carefully reasoned explanation of the importance of the

Fire Bowl at Bruneval. With the Prime Minister were members of the Cabinet and senior officers of the Armed Services. On the table in front of each man were copies of the fateful photographs, 68 and 69, and a typewritten report which the professor had spent most of the previous night writing.

There could be no mistake about the seriousness of the professor's speech. Every face in the room reflected deep anxiety. The whole future course of the war might be changed by the discovery of this Fire Bowl. The invasion itself, now being planned, might have to be postponed.

"In conclusion," the professor said, "it seems to me that we have only two alternatives as far as this installation is concerned. The first, and most obvious, is to send a large force of bombers and blow it to smithereens." He looked around the table with a faint smile. "But I'm afraid that wouldn't help us very much. The Germans would simply build another to replace it, protect it with more anti-aircraft guns; and we should still be in the dark as to the exact nature of their radar."

"What other course do you suggest?" the Prime Minister growled.

"Sir," Professor Cheswick said calmly, "as scientists, the only possible way in which we can decide about German radar is to examine it ourselves. We would have to tear it down, rebuild it, experiment with it, test it . . ."

"You mean," somebody cried, "you want to send a task force over to France to capture this apparatus and bring it back here?"

"Exactly," Professor Cheswick answered quietly.

"But that's fantastic! We can't send an invasion fleet to capture a few boxes of electronic gadgets!"

"Speaking again as a scientist," Professor Cheswick said, "that is what I propose. It is for the military experts to decide whether it's possible, and for those who make our policy to decide whether it's worth-while. We have been fortunate, incidentally, in bringing to this country a young Frenchman named Paul Martin, who watched the installation being built and who knows Bruneval like the back of his hand—"

A dozen voices rose in protest and query. "But . . ." "But . . ." "But . . ."

The Prime Minister intervened. "Gentlemen," he said, and the voices became silent. Every head turned toward him. His eyes were

gleaming, as if he had been gripped by some strange, fierce determination. "Gentlemen," he repeated, "it seems to me that we have here an opportunity for a magnificent adventure. Do we need this apparatus? Very well. We shall go and get it. We will snap our fingers at these Nazis. They think that they're the masters of Europe? This will be a splendid chance to show them that they are not, that the long arm of the Allied High Command can reach out to strike them wherever they hide."

Somebody said, "But, sir, at this time it would be difficult to assemble a large task force . . ."

"We already have the men to do the job," the Prime Minister said coolly. "Commandos."

"Commandos!"

The Prime Minister chuckled. "Professor, you shall have this Nazi apparatus. Now, tell me more about this young Frenchman. He sounds most interesting."

CHAPTER 8

Prepare for Action!

OR several days Paul saw very little of the English countryside. He lived, with Gaston, in a small Nissen hut about a hundred yards away from the main buildings of Intelligence Headquarters. In this hut he slept and ate his meals, hardly leaving it. When he did so Gaston accompanied him, like his shadow. To avoid difficulties he wore an R.A.F. uniform with the shoulder patch of the Free French Air Force; but instead of the usual R.A.F. forage cap he wore a black beret. Gaston teased him about this. "You are unique, my son," he said. "You are the one and only member of the Junior Free French Air Force. As such, you are its general, colonel, major, captain, lieutenant, sergeant, corporal, head cook and bottle washer. I salute you, my general." Paul laughed. He was already devoted to Gaston, and Gaston to him. He enjoyed Gaston's jokes.

There was little time for joking, though. Every minute of the day was taken up with the Fire Bowl. Another plane had been sent over the installation and had returned with photographs that showed more details of the farm and the surrounding areas. These photographs had been enlarged tremendously and mounted on wooden boards. With Professor Cheswick and Squadron Leader Marshall, Paul went over them inch by inch. He was very quick at learning how to identify the various landmarks. At first the photographs were hopelessly confusing—a crisscross of

black and white lines, odd gray shapes that
fitted together like a jigsaw puzzle, and blobs
that seemed to mean absolutely nothing.

Soon, though, he began to see that it all had
definite meaning. He discovered which lines
indicated roads and which indicated trenches
carrying power or telephone cables. The odd
gray jigsaw pieces were fields which had been
plowed at different times or were growing
various kinds of crops. The vague dark blobs
were woods; a light blob resolved itself under
the stereoscope as a house or factory. A black
blob might be a lake.

The experts could see all these things at a
glance; they could immediately pick out some
unusual object, measure it, and in a little
while describe its size and its purpose. They
could even tell which crops were growing in
the fields, or how recently the fields had been
plowed. Yet Paul could tell them things about
Bruneval that they could never learn from
photographs; things invaluable to their purpose. For example, in this spot there was a
small area of broken land. Yes, Paul could say

with authority: it's rocky and some of the rocks are big enough to conceal four or five men. Here there was a white scratch on a photograph, identified by Squadron Leader Marshall as a ditch. Yes, Paul explained, it is about five feet deep, about thirty feet long, sometimes muddy and very slippery, but I climbed through it the other day and the mud was frozen solid . . . The house on the cliffs? Yes, in the photograph you see two sides, with all the windows intact, but at the back of the house the windows are arranged differently and one or two are broken. The machine-gun posts? In these the guns face toward the sea but these face in a different direction. . . .

This was only the beginning. Working day and night, a number of technicians constructed large-scale models of the farm, accurate in every detail. Paul found it fascinating to watch the work growing under these men's skilled hands. On one large board they built the house on the cliffs, the Fire Bowl standing in the shallow pit, each machine-gun emplacement in its exact position. Looking

down at it Paul felt like Gulliver looking
down at the land of Lilliput. He could almost
see the Nazis marching stiffly to and from the
house and hear the thump of their heavy
boots.

Why, he asked himself sometimes, were the
Allies going to all this trouble? He had not
been told of the meeting in the Cabinet Room
at 10 Downing Street, nor what had been decided there. And he couldn't help wondering
what all this activity meant. He was intelligent enough to realize that if the Fire Bowl
was a great menace to Allied planes it would
not be too difficult to destroy it. A dozen
bombers concentrating on the area could send
it sky-high. But why, in that case, build such
painstakingly accurate models? Why, on these
huge photographs, so carefully mark every
rock, every tree, every path?

Then one day a swarm of officers arrived to
examine the photographs and the models.
They were from all the Services, Army, Navy
and Air Force, and they wanted to know
everything about Bruneval. What kind of

trees grew beside this ditch? What sort of beach was there under the cliffs? Sand? Pebbles? Were there any rocks near the beach that were covered at high tide? How many guns were there in this machine-gun emplacement? Was there a path through the woods at this point? Was the front door of the house made of wood? Metal? What about the back door?

The questions were endless. These officers wanted to know details that would make the farm and the Fire Bowl and the house on the cliffs as familiar to them as it all was to Paul. They wanted to be able to see it, touch it, feel it.

That evening, when the excitement had died down, Professor Cheswick came to Paul's hut, accompanied by Air Commodore Simpson. When they entered, Paul and Gaston stood to attention, but the air commodore motioned them to sit down.

"Paul," Professor Cheswick said, "your work on the Fire Bowl is nearly over now. Very soon I hope I shall be able to report great success as a result of all the help you've given

us. The work you've done has been invaluable. However, I want to talk to you now about yourself. I want to discuss your future."

Paul looked at him steadily.

"I've had plenty of opportunity," the professor went on, "to find out what a good brain you have and how well you apply it. We want boys like you. I should like to suggest that when you leave here you should complete your education at one of our best technical schools. Does this appeal to you?"

"Yes, sir," Paul said. "I should like to do that very much."

"Splendid. Well, then, think about it for the next few days and try to decide what particular subjects you'd like to take. Then we'll have another talk."

"Thank you, sir. I already know the subject I'd like to take most. Radar—"

"Good. Good."

"But first," Paul continued calmly, "I should like, if you please, to go with the expedition you are planning to send to Bruneval."

Air Commodore Simpson gave a loud gasp.

Professor Cheswick smiled. "I thought you'd guess what was going on, Paul."

"An expedition is going to France!" Gaston cried, leaping to his feet excitedly. "Without *me!* But that is impossible!"

"Sit down, Sergeant," the air commodore snapped.

Gaston shriveled at the order and said meekly, "Yes, sir. I beg your pardon, sir."

The air commodore turned sharply to Paul. "Who gave you the idea that we're sending an expedition to Bruneval, young man? Has anybody been talking to you?"

"Nobody in particular, sir," Paul replied politely. "But all the questions today, about the beach and the paths through the woods, made me think that perhaps an expedition was being planned."

"Quite right," Professor Cheswick smiled. "I should have been very surprised if you hadn't guessed, after all the recent activity in which you've been involved." The smile left his face and his voice became grave. "But I'm afraid your request is impossible, Paul, even though it does you great credit."

"Why is it impossible, sir?" Paul asked. By an immense effort he was just able to control his disappointment.

"Because this is war," the professor said. "We're planning to send an expedition to Bruneval, true; but the men we're sending over are some of our toughest soldiers—men who've been trained in the fiercest kind of

fighting. Commandos, Paul. Have you heard
of the commandos?"

"Yes, sir. All the same—"

"Listen, my boy. These men are hand-
picked for ruggedness and fighting spirit.
They've had months and months of hardening, the kind of hardening that would kill
most people. You simply couldn't keep up
with them. And besides that, it would be out
of the question to send a young boy on a raid
as dangerous as this one is bound to be."

"Sir," Paul said desperately, "you'll be
sending these commandos over at night, won't
you?"

The professor stared at him. "Perhaps."

"They *must* go at night, otherwise they will
be cut to pieces when they reach Bruneval.
But at night they might run into difficulties.
Even with all our photographs and all our
models, something might go wrong. Sir, I
know every little road and path around Bruneval, every rock and tree. I could get to the
Fire Bowl blindfolded. Let me go along as a
guide, in case they need my help."

"We couldn't do such a thing, Paul," Air Commodore Simpson said stiffly. "It's absolutely impossible."

"But if I could be of help!" Paul cried. "This expedition mustn't fail! Anything could happen in the darkness, and just by being there I might help if there's any trouble."

The air commodore looked at Professor Cheswick. Then he said to Paul, "Tell me once again, young man, exactly how old are you?"

"Eighteen, sir." In his heart Paul blessed Captain Dubois for giving him this one piece of advice.

"Eighteen, eh? Very good. You will hear in due course whether your request has been granted. In the meantime you will obey these orders I am giving to you: you will speak to nobody—and I mean *nobody*—about this conversation. You will not even mention the words Fire Bowl, or Bruneval, or commandos to a living soul, on pain of instant punishment. And that goes for you too, Sergeant."

"Yes, sir," Paul and Gaston said together.

The air commodore turned to Professor Cheswick. "And you want to send the lad to a technical school! A *school!* Why, the next thing you'll know is that he's crawling around on all fours with a knife between his teeth. Come along, my learned friend. We'd better leave here before the boy talks us into something we might regret."

The two men left. When the door had closed behind them, there was silence in the hut. Then Gaston leaped up and seized Paul by the shoulder. "My little general! You have brains in your head! You surprised them, you worried them! They have gone away thinking hard about us now! Who knows? Anything might happen next! You and I might set foot on the sacred soil of France before the next moon!"

Something happened the following morning.

A corporal came to the hut and said, "Camp Commandant's orders. Both of you will pack your kits and be ready to leave in half an hour."

"Leave for where?" Gaston cried.

The corporal looked him straight in the eyes. "The destination is secret, Sergeant. You'll find out all about it in due course. But I'll tell you this: I wouldn't go there for all the tea in China."

"Is that so?" Gaston said, and scratched his head thoughtfully.

The destination was secret enough—a commando training camp somewhere in the north of England. Paul and Gaston were wild with excitement when they discovered where they had been sent. In a little while, however, their enthusiasm became rather more restrained.

A sergeant greeted them on their arrival at the camp, a short square man who looked as if he had been hacked out of solid concrete. He said without any preliminaries, "You two men have come here to do six months' training in eight days. It can't be done, but at least we're going to try. Now, to start with, I'm supposed to look after your welfare. Are you hungry?"

"We haven't eaten since breakfast, Sergeant," Gaston said.

"Okay. Follow me to the canteen. I hope you aren't tired, by the way, after your long journey?"

"Not very tired, Sergeant," Paul said.

"That's good," the sergeant said, "because the canteen is twelve miles away, and we're going to run there. Incidentally, I notice that you don't have rifles. You can't run without rifles, you know. Let's go and get them." He sprinted off, and Paul and Gaston sprinted feverishly after him. Then, loaded down with full kit, they set off on their first commando route march.

The sergeant had not exaggerated. He ran most of the twelve miles to the canteen, which was on another camp. When they reached it, Paul and Gaston could scarcely drag one foot after the other.

They ate slabs of dry bread and stale cheese and drank mugs of hot cocoa. Then the sergeant said briskly, "You'd better get some sleep now. Reveille is at four-thirty."

"In the morning?" Gaston gasped in horror.

"Yes. Any other questions?"

Gaston swallowed. "Where do we sleep, Sergeant?"

"Please yourself," the sergeant answered indifferently. "You can curl up on the floor in the next room, if you like. It's empty and nobody will disturb your sweet dreams. Or if you're feeling really tough you can dig yourself a cosy little foxhole out-of-doors and bed down there. I'm not particular." He strode out, leaving Gaston pale and openmouthed.

"Is this possible?" Gaston whispered. "I have been in this war since 1939 and I have met many sergeants, but I have never met anybody so inhuman, so callous, so brutal—"

Paul walked wearily into the next room, sat down with his back to the wall and said, "We can't complain, Gaston. We asked for it." He had barely enough strength to say these words. His eyes closed and he flopped over like a rag doll. Gaston fell asleep still muttering to himself, "This is how they intend to stop us going to Bruneval. They are trying to kill us . . ."

They were awake again before dawn. Breakfast consisted of thick porridge, a few scraps of bacon, bread and strong tea. Then they were out trailing after the sergeant once more, following him through dense woods, scrambling up cliffs, wading through icy streams—neck-high in the water, with their rifles held over their heads.

"This is beginner's stuff," the sergeant explained when they stopped for ten minutes' rest. "I'm starting you off easy." He suddenly flung his rifle at Gaston with all his strength, and Gaston just managed to catch it, quivering with astonishment at this unexpected new attempt to kill him. "Good," the sergeant said. "You're supposed to stay on your toes even when you're resting. The enemy might throw anything at you, any minute of the day. Give me back that rifle."

By eight o'clock that night Paul and Gaston were asleep, stretched out on wooden boards that now seemed as comfortable as feather beds. An hour later the sergeant was blowing a whistle in their ears, abusing them for being such sluggards. Half-dead, they dressed, seized their rifles, stumbled out and followed him blindly through the darkness. They forded a river, clambered over barbed-wire fences, sprang at sacks that were meant to represent Nazi sentries, galloped through marshes until Paul felt that he would drop in his tracks with fatigue. But like most human beings his body had deep reserves of strength, deeper than he knew; and he was only just beginning to learn what his limits of endurance were. Besides this, his healthy life in the country had prepared him to some extent for this terribly hard training.

It was not hard, though, in comparison with the training the real commandos received. Paul saw some of the squads at work, crawling through a hail of live bullets from concealed machine guns, practicing attacks on enemy positions through exploding bombs. He saw them exercising with eight-inch logs on their shoulders, setting off on grueling route marches that might take five days and nights without rest. A troop of commandos might come off duty late in the afternoon, after a day of strenuous activity, and be told that they had to parade at dawn the next morning at some place a hundred miles away; and how they reached it was entirely their own business. There were no complaints. The men seemed to take pride, Paul saw, in every moment of hardship. Each man strove at all times to do more than his best.

So it went on for Paul and Gaston. Route marches by day and night, obstacle races over barbed wire and fortified stockades, cliff-climbing, weapon practice, physical exercises. Sleep was something that they snatched in periods of twenty minutes or half an hour; food was something they ate and drank while they marched. Could anybody survive such a routine?

They did. At the end of the eight days the sergeant grinned at them and said, "You're a couple of good lads. Don't kid yourselves that you're commandos now, because you aren't. But you ought to know how to look after yourselves if you get into a spot of trouble. Come back sometime when you have six months to spare and I'll finish the job. In the meantime, good luck to you both."

"It's been a pleasure," Gaston sighed.

"Thank you, Sergeant," Paul said. "This has been an experience I shall never forget."

They were sore in every muscle when they left the camp; but, curiously enough, they walked like commandos—very lithely, as if on tiptoe, and the heavy kitbags on their shoulders felt as if they were filled with feathers.

CHAPTER 9

The Commandos Go In

THE DATE was the twenty-seventh of February, 1942. The time was late evening. The place was the briefing room of an airfield in the south of England. The commandos stood around quietly, facing the huge aerial photographs of Bruneval and the scale models of the farm, the house on the cliffs and the Fire Bowl. They were calm and relaxed. Nobody could have guessed that in a few hours they would be storming through enemy-occupied territory like fiends.

Paul, standing among them with Gaston at his side, looked at them with admiration. In the past few days he had lived with them very closely; he knew them all by their first names, and they had accepted him as one of themselves. He had taken part in the many rehearsals for the raid; he had gone out on exercises, led by Major Cowles who was to be in command of the raiding parties; he had eaten with these men, slept in a hut with them, and listened to their talk. They did not act or talk like supermen, he discovered. They seemed, in fact, to be extraordinarily mild and easygoing. But under that mildness was tremendous alertness; under that easygoing manner was great confidence in themselves and their comrades. They knew the strength of their combined striking power.

By now both Paul and Gaston had recovered from the effects of those eight nightmarish days of training. As the sergeant had warned, they were not commandos now; by comparison with the men in this room they were still rather like children. Even so, their bodies had hardened; they had learned that in an emergency they could call on hidden reserves of endurance. They felt alive and full of energy, as if they had just returned from a long vacation, instead of from one of the most rugged training camps in the world. They both felt that this night was going to be the greatest experience of their lives.

There was a rustle of interest as Major Cowles entered the room, followed by Professor Cheswick and Air Commodore Simpson. The major, a tall broad-shouldered man, began to speak without any introduction. His voice was quiet, and he stood with one hand comfortably in his pocket.

"All of you know your jobs tonight," he began. "I'm only going to run over the operation briefly in case there are any last-minute questions."

He pointed to the Fire Bowl on the scale model.

"First, let me state again what it's all about.

The Nazis have developed this device, known as radar, which is a definite menace to all our future plans. We could destroy it, but that wouldn't help us very much. We want to capture various parts of it intact, so that our scientific experts can examine it in detail. This is your primary objective. We also need to capture a few of the Nazi technicians who operate this radar, since they might give us some useful information; that's your secondary objective.

"Furthermore, this is a historic occasion. It's the first invasion, in force, of France since the Germans drove us back at Dunkirk in 1940. And we want to make it good. We are going to strike panic into the hearts of the Nazis and encourage our good allies the French. From now on the Nazis are going to realize that they are not safe anywhere.

"Now, as to details. You will fly in Whitley bombers and be dropped over the target area at midnight. The assembly point, which you will all try to reach immediately, is the ditch you see on the photograph here. Our young friend Paul Martin has described it to you very exactly. It's in the cover of a row of trees on the edge of the woods.

"You will be in three groups, each under its own leader. The first group will storm the house on the cliffs and deal with any Nazi troops found there.

"The second group is the technical group. These men will capture the radar post and dismantle it.

"The third group will clear the way to the beach, opening up the way for our return.

"When the beach path is open, all three groups will assemble on the beach and give the signal to be taken off. Landing craft will come in for this purpose. These will be covered by other landing craft that will guard your withdrawal. Covering these, in turn, will be motor gunboats and two destroyers, so that you will be well protected on the return journey. These naval forces, incidentally, are already on their way to Bruneval and have reported that they are making good progress. Are there any questions?"

There were none.

Air Commodore Simpson stepped forward and said in his brisk manner, "I want to say a word about the flight arrangements. It's a perfect flying night: not much wind, a bright moon with a little cloud. Visibility should be good, and your pilots shouldn't have much difficulty finding the dropping area. You can expect some flak as you cross the French coast, but it will be light, I hope, and shouldn't give you any real trouble. We are also sending some planes to make a raid on a nearby area, which will draw off the enemy fighter planes located around Bruneval. I trust, therefore, that you'll have a comfortable trip."

Finally, Professor Cheswick stepped forward. He said with a chuckle, "I think this is the first time that science has had the help of a group of experts like yourselves. This is a piece of research that will go down in scientific textbooks as well as history books. That's all I have to say, and God bless every one of you."

"Thank you, Professor," Major Cowles said. He looked at his watch. "Zero hour for take-off is in fourteen and a half minutes. You'd better get ready, men."

The professor came hurrying toward Paul and said, "How do you feel, my boy?"

Paul smiled at him cheerfully. "Fine, sir. I'm very happy that I shall be in France again soon, even if it's only for a short while."

"Take care of yourself," the professor said. "Remember, I have great plans for you when you come back." He turned to Gaston. "I'm relying on you to look after this lad, Sergeant. See that he doesn't get into any real trouble."

"Yes, sir," Gaston answered solemnly. "I'll keep an eye on him."

"Sir," Paul asked, "will the Resistance take any part in this raid tonight?"

"No," Professor Cheswick replied. "Not this time. We've warned them to stay in hiding, because there's too much danger of reprisals. But the day is fast coming when they'll take a full part in our raids. Don't worry about this now, Paul. Just be sure to come back safely."

*   *   *   *   *

The commandos were rubbing burnt cork on their faces and hands, leaving a thick black grime that would stay on for hours. They wore paratroopers' crash helmets and they all carried heavy commando knives and hand grenades. Many of them had Sten guns—short light Tommy guns that could pour out a terrifying hail of fire; some had automatic pistols.

They were in very high spirits, laughing and joking as if they were going on an easy night exercise, not on a highly dangerous mission against the enemy.

They rocked with laughter as they saw Paul and Gaston cautiously applying the burnt cork, and they crowded round the two Frenchmen giving advice. At last Gaston grinned at Paul, "Eh, my little general! Even your own mother wouldn't recognize you now."

Paul grinned back, "And you, Sergeant, all you need is a banjo to make your fortune in a circus."

"You look like a real desperado," Gaston chuckled. "A bandit of the worst order."

"I should hate to meet you on a dark night," Paul retorted. "You would frighten any respectable person out of his skin."

They were both armed with commando knives, but Paul had no gun. Gaston had both a Sten gun and a revolver.

The order came to assemble outside the briefing room, and the commandos trooped out and formed into squads in the darkness.

Nearby, Paul could hear the sputter and whine of aircraft engines, bursting into shattering roars as they warmed up. As he stood at attention his hands were tightly clenched and he could feel his heart beating rapidly. He was cold, but not with fear. It was like the line-up before a football game, when his body always tightened with expectation. He began to relax in a few moments, and he smiled to himself at the excitement of this adventure. He could never have imagined it in his wildest dreams; yet here he was, one of a company of commandos setting off for France . . .

Then the darkness was split by a noise like the screeching of a thousand cats in agony. His blood froze; but at his side Gaston exclaimed, "Bagpipes!" Before Paul could get over his astonishment at the unearthly sound, his squad was marching toward the waiting planes.

The pipers led the way, stepping out at a steady pace, their pipes skirling Scottish songs that Paul had never heard before; but in some mysterious way the shrill sounds seemed to creep into his veins and made him tingle. It was the music of savage warriors, a noise that heartened men going into battle and terrified the enemy.

With the precision of guardsmen on a parade ground, the commandos marched around the perimeter of the airfield, and as each squad reached its plane it wheeled smartly. The pipes were still playing as the men entered the Whitleys. Paul found himself sitting on a narrow bench that ran along the side of the fuselage; with him was an almost unrecognizable Gaston and a horde of black-faced, grinning commandos. It seemed completely unreal. Then he heard the twin motors of the Whitley speed up and felt the plane lurch as it began its slow waddle to the runway.

"Hold tight," Gaston said in his ear, and gripped his arm. The noise of the motors grew louder and louder, the plane seemed to be moving at incredible speed, and then all sensation ceased. He might have been sitting in an armchair in his own home. There was a cheer from the men, and Gaston's hold loosened.

An officer came over to Paul and looked down at him with a smile. "How are you feeling, laddie?"

"Fine, sir. Just fine."

"Try to get a little sleep. We shan't reach the French coast until shortly before midnight."

Some of the commandos were singing. Some were playing cards. Gaston brought two sleeping bags from a pile in the rear of the plane and handed one to Paul. "Curl up in this, my general. Make yourself comfortable."

"Thank you," Paul said. He lay curled up warmly, suspended in space, lulled by the steady purring of the motors, thinking of Bruneval, which he was about to visit in this strange way, thinking of his father and mother, of Theo, of the Resistance girl Denise, of Captain Dubois and the skipper of the *Dauphin*. How exciting everything is, he thought vaguely, and his mind wandered off into a pleasant fog.

The next thing he knew Gaston was shaking him. "Put on your parachute," Gaston said. "We're nearly there."

Paul scrambled out of his sleeping bag, tightened his helmet and fastened his parachute. Gaston checked it, pulling at the various straps to make certain they were secure, and Paul did the same for him.

"Twenty minutes more," Gaston said, "and we shall be flying over our own country."

All the men were standing now, lined up at action stations. There was no tension, no sense that they were going into danger. They were simply waiting to descend from the plane to do an important job. The Whitley lurched suddenly, and somebody said in a steady voice, "Hold on, boys. Flak." It lurched again and seemed to tip over slightly. The calm voice said again, "The Nazis have some flak-ships down there. We're taking evasive action."

"Paul," Gaston said urgently, "stay close to me all the time. Remember. Stay close!"

A red light came on. The pilot of the Whitley was turning into the target. The hole in the floor of the fuselage through which the commandos would drop was open. The first men were already in position, waiting for the green light which was the signal to jump. Paul had practiced the routine many times already; he knew exactly what was going to happen, but he was surprised at the speed with which it was happening now, in actual combat conditions.

There it was! The green light! The first men had dropped . . . the line was moving forward . . . Gaston was behind him holding on to his shoulder, and for some reason Paul could hear the shrill wailing of the bagpipes in his ears again. Suddenly he himself was sitting over the drop hole looking down into darkness—an R.A.F. sergeant had hooked up his static line—there was a whispered *go* and he was through the hole and his legs were blowing sideways as he was caught in the Whitley's slip stream. There was a jerk at his shoulder as the static cord pulled his parachute open, and he saw it billow out and rise over his head, blotting out the sky. Then he was floating in a black silent world, without any sensation of falling, until the earth rose up slowly to meet him. He landed on it—in the midst of a soft white coldness—with a thump, and found himself being dragged forward. He grabbed the shrouds of the parachute, fumbled with the catch to release it, and tumbled on his chest into a foot of snow, gasping but uninjured.

Bruneval! But was this Bruneval? He stood up cautiously and looked around him. Yes. The woods were over to his left, the farmhouse and the house on the cliffs and the Fire Bowl were ahead of him, hidden in the darkness. He could see the gray shapes of the commandos against the snow, crouching as they ran to the assembly point in the ditch, and then he heard Gaston's voice calling quietly, "Paul! Paul!"

He called back, "Gaston."

"*À moi,*" Gaston exclaimed. "*À moi!*" The traditional French cry of comrades in battle: "To me! To me!"

Paul found him quickly, only a few yards

away. "Are you all right?" Gaston asked anxiously, and Paul answered, "Yes."

"Let's get to the assembly point then. Hurry!"

They began to run. The snow blanketed all noise; the world seemed asleep. Even the throb of the Whitley bombers had dwindled. There was only this uncanny movement of silent men all running swiftly toward the ditch under the trees. Scattered over the snow were cylindrical containers holding additional equipment for the raid—guns, dynamite, signaling apparatus. These the commandos scooped up as they ran.

"France!" Gaston laughed. "My beautiful France!" He snatched up a handful of snow in his stride, and held it until it melted, as if it were something infinitely precious. Paul knew how he felt. Even in these tense moments he was overjoyed at being back in his own land; every tree, every stone in his path was familiar. He had walked with his father and mother here; played at boy's games with his friends;

and the recollection that the Nazis had occupied it made him burn with anger.

"Here's the ditch," he panted to Gaston. For one awful moment he thought that it was empty, that some mistake had been made and the commandos had gone somewhere else. But then he saw the black-faced men crouching on their haunches, waiting motionless for the order that would send them into action; and he slipped quietly down among them.

"Here's Paul," somebody whispered, and he heard his name going down the line. "Paul . . . Paul . . . Paul." Then the whispering came back to him. The commando at his side touched his arm and muttered in his ear, "Squeeze past me, son. Report to Major Cowles."

This was no time for questions. He obeyed the order immediately, edging past the men until he reached the major.

"Paul Martin reporting, sir," he whispered.

"Paul!" the major said. "Thank God you're safe. Now, listen. We go into action in three minutes. But all our men aren't here yet. I've

just had a report that two of the Whitleys were
driven off course by the flak and dropped their
squads somewhere to the southwest, behind
the woods. These were the men who had the
job of clearing the way to the beach. They
were expected to wipe out the machine-gun
posts on the cliffs. Without them we may be
cut off. Do you understand?"

"Yes, sir."

"It's possible that they're lost in the woods.
This is what I want you to do, Paul. Stay here
while we go forward. If these troops haven't
arrived by the time you hear firing, go into the
woods and find them. It's vitally important
that they find their way to the cliffs. If those
defenses aren't knocked out we'll never get
down to the beach."

Paul's heart began to beat fast. He had
known it all along. He had known that he
could be of help to the commandos on this
mission; and here was his chance.

CHAPTER 10

Attack on the Fire Bowl

"O NE minute to go," the major said almost
under his breath. He was staring at the
sweep-second hand of his illuminated
watch. "Fifty-five ... fifty ... forty-five ..."

There was not a sound from the crouching
commandos. Paul held his breath.

"Thirty ... twenty-five ... twenty ..."

Paul's hands were clenched behind his back.

160

In his mind's eye he could see the machine guns bristling out of the emplacements that guarded the Fire Bowl, he could see the Nazis waiting in their dugouts, peering into the darkness for any sign of danger, never expecting that danger was so near.

"Ten seconds . . . five . . ."

The major blew his whistle, a muted rattle like the choked, angry sound of a hawk about to pounce. That was all. Without any other order the major crept out of the ditch and went running toward the house on the cliffs. Ranged on either side of him were the hunched, threatening figures of the commandos. And still there was no sound—no sound of clattering footsteps, no sound of clinking guns.

Then all the figures disappeared into the night. Paul, left alone, felt as if he had dreamed the attack had begun. The commandos seemed to have vanished utterly, like ghosts.

These first few minutes were critical. If the attack were discovered too soon the machine guns would open fire, mowing down and perhaps halting the commandos. But there was still only silence. Total silence.

The Nazis guarding Bruneval felt at peace with themselves. Most of them were in the farmhouse, soundly asleep. Those others who were on duty were snug in their dugouts, and a little bored. There wasn't much to do, guarding this radar installation. After all, Germany was the undisputed master of Europe now, and there was nothing to fear from the Allies. True, a few bombers had flown overhead about ten minutes before, probably on their way to bomb some luckless town in Germany; but these bombing raids were ineffectual, and the Nazi night fighters would deal with the interlopers. Had not Adolf Hitler himself declared that Europe was a fortress the enemy would never penetrate? Why didn't the stupid Allies realize they had lost the war? Why didn't they stop making foolish speeches about returning here? . . .

They sat in the machine-gun posts bored, half-asleep, waiting for their spell of duty to end so that they could go back to bed in the farmhouse and snore comfortably for a few hours...

The major had reached the house on the cliffs. Silently, his men surrounded it.

The second group of commandos had reached the Fire Bowl. This, too, was surrounded without a sound.

An instant later came the signal for attack— a fierce blast on the major's whistle. Now there was no time to waste, no further need to move in silence. He dashed up to the door of the house, found it open and rushed through. His men poured after him, guns and grenades ready to deal with any Nazi troops they found here. There were none in the rooms downstairs. The major went flying upstairs, shouting in a tremendous voice, "Surrender! Come out with your hands up!" A German soldier came out onto the landing, a rifle nervously in his hands, bewildered by this unexpected noise. Before he could fire, a bullet tore through his heart. He was the only occupant of the house, the major discovered. The Nazis had been so sure of themselves that they had not taken the trouble to put more than one man in it to guard it through the night.

Swiftly the major detailed a dozen commandos to hold the house. Since it stood between the farmhouse, where the main force of the Nazis slept, and the Fire Bowl, it could act as a barrier in case the Nazis attempted to fight. From the Fire Bowl itself came the dull explosions of grenades, and the major went speeding through the snow to discover what was happening there. Six Nazis had made a hopeless effort to defend the installation; grenades had killed five of them and the sixth had been captured after making an attempt to escape. The squad of technicians was already dismantling the apparatus, while a number of commandos stood alert outside. Pieces of the precious equipment, so vital to the Nazis and the Allies alike, were being carried out swiftly.

But at the road that led to the beach only a

handful of commandos lay concealed in the
darkness, waiting to destroy the six or seven
machine-gun posts that barred the way down.
There were not enough men to take the post.
They waited, hoping desperately that the re-
mainder of their section would arrive so that
they could launch their attack. Otherwise,
those machine guns could hold up the entire
raiding party long enough for the Nazi troops
in the farmhouse to come into action. Suddenly they heard the first staccato clatter from
the farmhouse—two machine guns firing errat-
ically into the night, unsure who or where the
attackers were, just firing blindly out of
windows.

The way to the beach *had* to be cleared.
Beyond the beach, a quarter of a mile out to
sea, were the landing craft and the motor gunboats and the destroyers, watching anxiously
for the signal to come in close to take the commandos off. Enemy destroyers and E-boats had
passed them on patrol, and had miraculously
missed them. But that, truly, was a miracle;
and the small fleet was in deadly danger every

moment it was stationary. If the commandos did not reach the beach soon, the Nazis would have sent out a general alert that would bring scores of their warships to this area. That would bring, too, land reinforcements which would seal off the beach forever.

At the first sound of firing Paul slipped out of the ditch and went quickly toward the woods. His only weapon was his heavy knife, and he loosened it in its sheath so that it would be ready for immediate use if necessary. His mind was working very clearly. After he had gone a little way he stopped, and stood with his head cocked forward, holding his breath. If the missing commandos had reached the woods he would hear some sound—the slight scrape of a boot against tall grass, the crackle of a branch underfoot.

He heard nothing. There was only the gentle sighing of the trees, laden down by snow.

He crept forward another hundred yards and listened again. Behind him he heard muffled shots; ahead, still nothing.

He reached the outskirts of the woods and began to work his way along them, toward the village where he had been born and had lived all his life. Then, in a low crouching rush, he went scurrying up a chalky bank that gave him enough height to look over the nearby fields, and stood straining ears and eyes to catch some sign of the missing men. It was a dangerous place. A roving Nazi patrol might easily have spotted him here. But his personal danger no longer mattered; all that mattered was getting those commandos in action against the beach defenses.

He waited for several minutes. The cold air was beginning to numb his body. Suddenly he thought he heard a tiny sound over to his left, and he stiffened. The sound was not repeated.

Now he realized that he was in double danger. The sound might have been made by a Nazi trailing after him, or by a commando tracking him down in the belief that he was a Nazi guard. He knew only too well how the commandos worked—creeping through the snow like cats, pouncing out of nowhere, kill-ing with a single knife-thrust. They couldn't be expected to know that Major Cowles had sent him out to find them.

Was the sound made by a Nazi or a commando? There was only one way to find out. He took a whistle from his pocket and blew it very gently, his hands cupped over it, making a noise that might be a bird or a small night-prowling animal.

He waited for a reply. None came.

He blew the whistle again in the same way, and repeated it in desperation. This time, clearly and decisively, a whistle answered. As soon as he heard it he went running down the bank, wildly calling out, "This way! This way!"

A voice snarled out of the darkness, "Who goes there?"

"Paul," he answered. "Paul," and stopped abruptly, realizing that the commandos would take no chances, that by now a dozen guns were leveled at him, ready to blast him into eternity if he made one false move.

A shadow wavered across the snow, followed

by other shadows. "Paul *who?*" the voice demanded. It came from another direction now.

"Paul Martin."

"What are you doing here?"

"Major Cowles sent me to lead you to the machine guns overlooking the beach. We heard that you were lost."

The voice laughed. Paul recognized it as belonging to a Scottish sergeant. "Och, Paul, and thank the Lord it's you, laddie. But ye took an awfu' risk standing in yon place. I nearly put a bullet through your handsome heid."

"There's no time to lose, Sergeant," Paul cried. "They've begun to attack the Fire Bowl."

The shadows had reached him, had materialized as men in familiar uniform. "Aye, Paul, we heard the firing," the sergeant said. "We were making our way toward it, through yonder gap in the trees—"

"No," Paul interrupted. "I can show you a short cut through the woods. We go this way."

The sergeant blew a short blast on his whistle. "At the double!" he shouted. There was no need now for silence. The commandos were going through, no matter who tried to stop them.

"Lead on," he said grimly to Paul. "They'll be needing us. Let's get there fast."

The machine-gun fire from the farmhouse was growing fiercer. Bewildered by the unexpected attack, unable to guess how the raiders had reached Bruneval, the Nazis were making a confused effort to defend themselves. The major and his men calmly returned the fire, lying flat in the snow. They were grouped around the Fire Bowl, protecting it, trying to give the technicians every second they needed to complete their job. Equipment had already begun to move toward the cliffs. Everything was going as planned, except the final and most urgent task of clearing the way down to the beach. The major wondered whether Paul had been successful in finding the missing commandos, what was happening in the woods . . .

In the distance, traveling along a road that led to the farm, Paul saw the dimmed lights of three cars. They must be bringing up reinforcements, he realized; and there might be more Nazis following. It couldn't be helped. His first duty was to protect the men who were dismantling and carrying off the all-important apparatus. He and his commandos would stay to the bitter end, if it came to that, and fight a delaying battle to allow the apparatus to be taken aboard the landing craft. This was the purpose of the raid. It was his duty to see that it was fulfilled.

But the technicians had worked fast and efficiently. A corporal, wriggling flat on his stomach, reached the major and reported cheerfully, "The last load is on its way to the cliffs, sir."

"Have you set the demolition charges to destroy everything that's left?"

"Yes, sir. They'll go off in about three minutes."

"Good."

The major's whistle blew for retreat. Still facing the farmhouse, the commandos began to move back steadily, blazing away from a dozen different directions, confusing the Nazis who must have felt by now that an entire Allied army had suddenly descended upon them. Their confusion was increased by the violent explosions under the Fire Bowl.

All that remained now was to get down to the beach and signal the waiting ships. But was the way clear? The major decided to find out for himself. He sprinted ahead, past the

piles of equipment, and reached the gap between steep cliffs that led down to safety. It
was dark here, and he could not see what the
position was. The machine-gun posts, concealed in shadow, were silent.

Were their crews dead? Had the guns been
knocked out?

He could not tell. His men were running
toward him, and he blew a short warning blast
on his whistle to halt them. Before anybody
made another move, he had to find out for certain what had happened.

The commandos halted warily at his command. Then, from the beach, a gruff voice
called, "Come on down. The boats are here.
It's all right."

"Come on, men," the major cried. "Hurry!"

They began to move, but as they did so a
voice called from the other side of the gap,
"Major! Get back! The beach isn't taken yet!
Get back!" At once, machine guns opened fire.
Two of the commandos fell.

"Flat on your faces!" the major bawled.
"It's a trap!"

The machine guns had opened fire a second too early. The commandos snaked back, their bodies pressed to the ground, taking with them their two wounded comrades.

Coldly, the major considered the situation. After all this, after achieving full success in dismantling the Fire Bowl and bringing the equipment as far as the cliff top, they might be completely halted by the machine guns defending the beach path. It was bitter.

He shouted across the gap, "How many men do you have over there?"

"Major, only half my section. Not enough to attack all the emplacements."

The major bit his lip. He needed every man he had on this side to fight off the Nazis from the farmhouse and their reinforcements. And yet these machine guns had to be wiped out.

"Sergeant!" he snapped.

"He's been wounded, sir," a commando replied from the shadows.

"Corporal!"

"Sir!"

"Take nine men to reinforce the section

across the gap. You will destroy the machine guns that fired on us."

"Yes, sir."

The major heard his men creep off and wondered what would happen now. You gave an order, *Destroy the guns,* and you could trust your men to try to carry out that order. But it might not work out. Forty men could do it in a swift maneuver, attacking from different directions; twenty might be massacred. That would make the situation even more desperate. If only Paul had managed to bring the missing men here in time!

In a couple of minutes the action would start. He waited tensely.

The Germans in the farmhouse had not yet made any move. They still seemed to be dazed, uncertain what had hit them, and a group of commandos was still keeping them occupied with accurate fire, preventing them from showing their heads. But that could only last a little while longer . . .

Then the major heard a shout, a wild sound that must have struck terror into the Nazis' hearts, *"Caber Feigh!"*—"The Antlers of the Deer!" The war cry of the Scottish Highlanders. The shout came nearer, and he laughed aloud, knowing what it meant.

"Here are your men," he called vehemently across the gap. "Wait for them! Wait for them!"

In the growing clamor another voice rang out. It was Gaston. "Paul!" he cried. *"À moi! À moi!"*

The battle for the machine guns was short. A horde of ferocious commandos went swarming over the cliff, Tommy guns blazing, hurling their grenades into the sandbagged emplacements where the Nazis cowered under this paralyzing attack, wiping the crews out before they had a chance to fire. In a great savage rush the black-faced men poured down to the beach, the Scots yelling their war cry, *"Caber Feigh! Caber Feigh!"* guns and grenades and the screams of the dying shattering the night.

Then, abruptly, it was over. A powerful

voice called exultantly, "The way is clear, Major," and then quietly, efficiently, the secrets of the Fire Bowl were carried down, and the commandos took their places under the shelter of the cliffs. From the beach, bright with moonlight, a signal flashed out to the waiting ships to come immediately.

Gaston was hugging Paul with joy. "I thought you were lost in those woods forever, my little general," he said. "I kept wondering what I should tell the professor when I returned."

"This is my own country," Paul said. "I couldn't get lost in it."

The major came over, still tense and yet pleased. "You did a wonderful job, Paul," he said. "We shouldn't be here now if those missing troops hadn't arrived in time."

"Did we get all the apparatus from the Fire Bowl, sir?" Paul asked earnestly.

"Everything we need, my lad."

"What about casualties, sir?"

"We lost one man. Two were wounded. But I've just made a quick check, and there are still seven missing. They belonged to the sections that were dropped away from the target area."

"Sir!" Paul cried. "Let me go back and find them."

The major said heavily, "No, Paul. I can't let you take another chance like that. You've already done your part."

There was a cry, "Sir! The boats are coming in!"

Grinding into the shallow water came the monstrous shapes of the landing craft, carrying fresh troops who could cover the commandos' withdrawal. A cheer went up as the ramps were lowered.

"Paul," the major ordered. "Get on board. Go with him, Sergeant."

Neither Paul nor Gaston dared to disobey the order. They waded into the icy water and clambered up the ramp of the nearest boat. Following them came three disheveled Nazi prisoners, and commandos carrying the secrets of the Fire Bowl. Too late, some guns opened up from the cliff top; but the guns mounted on the landing craft answered with a torrent of fire that silenced them.

There was no further opposition. A minute later the landing craft backed away and trundled out to sea, to the waiting warships. The raid was over. Triumphantly, the flotilla made for England.

In the warmth of a cabin, wrapped in blankets and still faithfully guarded by Gaston, Paul fell asleep.

He dreamed of Bruneval, which he was now leaving again for the second time.

He dreamed of Bruneval, peaceful, quiet, free of the Nazis. In his dream he saw green grass growing where the Fire Bowl had been, and wild flowers. Not only Bruneval but the whole of France was free; the people could laugh and talk as they pleased; the invader had been defeated and driven out. And in this dream somebody was talking to him.

It was the commando major saying, "You did your part," and Paul smiled in his sleep.